W9-CGM-273

Dylan shouted from the hall. "What the devil are you doing in there?"

The last thing Glory wanted was for him to see the room before it was completely finished.

"Just having a new light fixture hung," she said, joining him. "Is there something you needed?"

"Yeah, you."

Glory's breath caught and she stared at him. She felt warm deep inside.

"There's some delivery guy downstairs" he said, frowning. "I need his truck out of my way, now."

It took Glory a few beats to catch up. She felt like a fool. "Of course," she said, hoping her voice didn't wobble. "I'll get the guys to unload it now."

"Good." Dylan turned and bounded down the stairs, leaving Glory wishing she could stop the lustful thoughts she was having about him. Dylan wasn't interested in her. Except for a few rare moments, he'd been nothing but cold and unreachable. But as she called to the boys to come help, it took more concentration than it should have to slow the pounding of her heart.

Dear Reader,

My great-aunt and her husband lived in a house that had been built in the 1890s. He was born there in 1900 and lived there all his life, until the two of them moved into town to live in the nursing home. They're gone now, but the house still stands at the curve in the county road, a reminder to me of summer visits and holidays spent with cousins and relatives of all ages.

There was something about that grand Victorian farmhouse, handed down from one generation to the next, that fascinated me. With tall ceilings and transom windows over the doorways, a beautiful wood staircase enclosed in a room of its own and the two triangular porches where family often sat and enjoyed the summer evenings, it enthralled me each time we visited.

When it came time to write about Dylan Walker's home, a large old farmhouse that had been passed down from one generation to the next, my aunt and uncle's house couldn't have been more perfect. Join Dylan and Glory as they learn just how even the saddest of memories can become the best.

Best wishes and happy reading!

Roxann

Designs on the Cowboy
ROXANN DELANEY

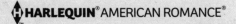

If you purchased this book without a cover you should be aware that this book is stolen property. It was reported as "unsold and destroyed" to the publisher, and neither the author nor the publisher has received any payment for this "stripped book."

Recycling programs
for this product may
not exist in your area.

ISBN-13: 978-0-373-75459-5

DESIGNS ON THE COWBOY

Copyright © 2013 by Roxann Farmer

All rights reserved. Except for use in any review, the reproduction or utilization of this work in whole or in part in any form by any electronic, mechanical or other means, now known or hereafter invented, including xerography, photocopying and recording, or in any information storage or retrieval system, is forbidden without the written permission of the publisher, Harlequin Enterprises Limited, 225 Duncan Mill Road, Don Mills, Ontario M3B 3K9, Canada.

This is a work of fiction. Names, characters, places and incidents are either the product of the author's imagination or are used fictitiously, and any resemblance to actual persons, living or dead, business establishments, events or locales is entirely coincidental.

This edition published by arrangement with Harlequin Books S.A.

For questions and comments about the quality of this book, please contact us at CustomerService@Harlequin.com.

® and TM are trademarks of Harlequin Enterprises Limited or its corporate affiliates. Trademarks indicated with ® are registered in the United States Patent and Trademark Office, the Canadian Trade Marks Office and in other countries.

Printed in U.S.A.

HARLEQUIN®
www.Harlequin.com

ABOUT THE AUTHOR

Roxann Delaney doesn't remember a time when she wasn't reading or writing, and she always loved that touch of romance in both. A native Kansan, she's lived on a farm, in a small town and has returned to live in the city where she was born. Her four daughters and grandchildren keep her busy when she isn't writing or designing websites. The 1999 Maggie Award winner is excited to be a part of the Harlequin American Romance line and loves to hear from readers. Contact her at roxann@roxanndelaney.com or visit her website, www.roxanndelaney.com.

Books by Roxann Delaney
HARLEQUIN AMERICAN ROMANCE

In memory of Aunt Dorothy and Uncle Milt Harrington.

Chapter One

"So this is how you honor the memory of our parents."

Dylan Walker didn't bother to look up from the melting ice cube floating in the glass of amber liquid he held. Nobody but his sister talked to him that way. Because she was eleven months older than him, she thought she had the right. He usually disagreed, but at that moment, he didn't care.

"Nice of you to drop by, Erin."

The sound of her boot heels on the old linoleum kitchen floor grew closer. "I had a feeling it had come to this," she said.

He detected a note of sadness in her voice, but ignored it. "It's no big deal to have a drink, now and then."

"It is when now and then becomes every day."

"You don't know what you're talking about."

"I do know. You and I have been running from the same devil for all these years. It's time to stop."

Slamming the glass down on the table in front of him, he got to his feet. Although he was a little unsteady, he wasn't going to let it stop him from saying what he needed to say. "I got through it this year, Erin. I stayed here and rode it out."

In the pale glow from the yard light outside the window, he saw her nod. "I know. Luke told me. But look at yourself now. Just what kind of victory was it?"

The truth was almost more than he could take. He wanted to sit down, but he knew that if he did, she'd win. "One step at a time," he said, without trying to hide the belligerence in his voice.

She shook her head. "You've taken one step forward and two steps back."

"I'm better!" His voice seemed to bounce off the walls of the old house, taunting him, but he wouldn't give in.

"Saying it doesn't make it so."

Squeezing his eyes shut, he prayed his temper wouldn't get the best of him. When he felt more in control, he opened them to find his sister standing next to him. He towered over her more than a foot, but he knew from the stubborn glint in her eyes that she wasn't going to put up with any of his excuses.

Her gaze bored a hole in him as she tipped her head back to look up at him. "You've got to let it go, Dylan. You were a kid. You can't keep blaming yourself for the accident."

He'd never forget the day his parents died. "They were on their way to town because of me."

A strange look flashed over her face, and he thought he saw a slight shake of her head. "It doesn't matter. That was then. This is now."

"But it does—"

"Here's what you're going to do," she continued, leaving no room for argument. "You're going to clean yourself up and fix up this house."

He managed a shrug. "A shower and some paint will do that."

She didn't even blink an eye. "Since I can't count on

you to do even that, I've hired someone who'll be here in a few days to do what needs to be done."

He wouldn't let her get away with this. "And what if I refuse?"

The silence in the room was almost unbearable as she stared at him. "If you think I'm joking about this, Dylan, go ahead and try me. But here's what's going to happen if you don't agree. I'll put the house up for sale, and you can go do whatever it is you want to do with your life, even if it's nothing. You just won't be doing it here."

He couldn't believe it. "You're kidding."

"If that's what you think, you're more out of touch than I thought. You can either stay here during the renovations that will make this house become something we can all be proud of again, or you can start looking for another place to live. I'm not going to let the memory of our parents become nothing but a run-down old house."

"You wouldn't throw me out."

Her eyes were hard and unforgiving, and her mouth was set in an angry, thin line. "I wouldn't try testing that if I were you."

Before he could think of some kind of stinging response, she'd turned to walk out the kitchen door and into the night.

"She wouldn't dare," he said, sinking to his chair. At least he didn't think so.

But by the next morning, he wasn't so sure Erin wouldn't do exactly what she'd said she would. His sister had a mean streak that rarely showed itself, but he'd seen it last night. He hadn't been at his mental best then, but now that he was thinking more clearly, he knew better than to take her threat lightly. And all he could do was wonder and wait for whoever it was she'd hired to show up.

He hadn't noticed a vehicle driving into the yard the next morning, but he heard a knock on the door of the screened-in porch off the kitchen as he sat drinking his morning coffee. "It's open," he called out.

"Dylan?"

He looked up at the sound of the female voice to find a pretty blonde woman he hadn't seen since high school standing in his doorway. Clearing his throat, he stood and searched for something to say. "Yeah, it's me" was the only thing that came to mind.

"And looking just the same as you did in high school," she said, with a smile he'd never forgotten. "You need to bottle your secret."

He couldn't believe he was having a conversation with Glory Caldwell. Or Glory Caldwell *Andrews,* he quickly corrected. The most popular girl in school, who'd been head cheerleader, Prom Queen and so many other things, actually remembered him. And he'd been…well, he'd been nobody special and never thought she knew he existed.

"What is it you have there?" She stepped inside the kitchen and picked up the paint samples he'd grabbed at Mercer's Hardware the day before. "Paint chips?"

It was the reminder he needed to come to his senses. When he did, it was clear to him why Glory was standing in his house. "You're the one Erin hired?"

Glory nodded. "Did she tell you how excited I am to have this opportunity? I've always loved your house. It's so big and grand—"

"You remember it?" He couldn't think of any reason she would.

Her cornflower-blue eyes widened. "Anybody who's

been around Desperation for very long knows the Walker place. Besides, you and I went all through school together. It isn't as if we're strangers."

He wasn't quite sure how to take that. As far as he knew, they might as well have been strangers. But he couldn't very well tell her that.

"You don't believe me, do you?"

His answer was a shrug. He'd forgotten as much of his childhood as he could. "I really don't remember."

"I do. I remember watching you play baseball from the time we were kids."

She did? He had a hard time believing it, but he'd never thought she was someone who said things just so people would like her.

"And you were good. Don't you forget that, Dylan Walker."

"Thanks." But he didn't mention that he hadn't had a glove on his hand or thrown a ball for fifteen years. Nor would he ever again.

She pointed at the paint chips. "You understand that I can do much more than brush on a little paint, don't you?"

He looked at the Creamy Ivory and Oyster samples, and all he saw was white.

"There's so much you can do these days with color," she said when he didn't answer.

"Is that so?"

"Oh, yes!" She ducked her head as her cheeks turned a soft pink. "I'm sorry," she said, looking up at him from under her lashes. "It's just that, well, I'm so excited to have the job of redecorating your home."

"Yeah? So you have some ideas?"

"Maybe a few."

He thought about it. She'd probably do a good job,

but he had a bad feeling about the whole thing. He just couldn't put his finger on what it was or why. "I'll be honest here, Glory," he said, trying to think of the best way to tell her he didn't want her there. "None of this was my idea."

Seconds ticked by before she spoke. "I understand." Reaching into the big bag that hung from her shoulder, she frowned and shook her head. "I have a— Ah, here it is," she said, pulling out a card. Instead of handing it to him, she walked around the table to where he stood. Smiling, she stuck the card in his shirt pocket. "Just let me know when I can start."

He watched her turn and walk out the door. He didn't want Glory Andrews in his house and should have told her not to bother coming back. But her arrival proved to him that his sister would stick by her word. He really didn't have a choice. He would have to let Glory do whatever it was his sister had hired her to do.

After picking up his cup and taking another drink of coffee, he pulled out the card she'd put in his pocket and looked at it.

Glory Be Antiques and Decorating.

GLORY STOOD AT the window of the shop, looking out at the town she'd left behind almost fifteen years before. Things had changed more than she'd expected them to, but from what she could tell since returning to town two weeks ago, it was still the Desperation she remembered.

It wasn't only the town that she was thinking about, but her encounter with Dylan Walker four days earlier. Never, never had she *ever* used feminine tricks to lure anyone—especially a man—into doing something she wanted. But it couldn't be helped. She'd promised his sister, who had warned her that he wouldn't be receptive, that she would find a way to get Dylan to agree to let her restore and redecorate the house where Erin and her two brothers had grown up. Erin had explained that it needed some updating, but she didn't trust Dylan to do it, much less do it right.

She hadn't heard anything from Dylan since then, and she was beginning to worry. Erin was counting on her—and had paid her a hefty retainer she desperately needed. Even so, she didn't feel right about barging into the house and taking over without his approval. And she sure hadn't gotten that.

The sound of footsteps coming down the old wooden stairs that led to the upper floor of the building dragged her back to the present. Pushing her apprehension about the job aside, she hoped she didn't appear worried.

"Did I hear the door?"

Putting a smile on her face, Glory turned around. "It was me, Gram. I stepped out for a little fresh air." She hated having to tell a lie, but it couldn't be helped. She didn't want Gram to worry. "Did you find what you were looking for up there?"

Louise Gardner, wearing a pair of denim pants and an old shirt, appeared from behind a dusty curtain hiding the short hallway that led to the stairs. "No, but I found a lot of other things."

"Is that good or bad?"

Her grandmother smiled and touched her light-colored graying hair. "Oh, I suspect it's good. I'd forgotten your grandfather took to storing so much up there. Now that you've decided to open up an antiques shop along with your decorating, you won't have to go looking for nearly as much to fill it with."

"That *is* good news. If I don't have to go out hunting for items to resell, it'll save me time *and* money. So where do we start?"

"It's up to you," Louise said with a shrug. "We could go through what's upstairs and weed out what's good and what would be better thrown away."

Glory moved to stand by the wood-burning stove that had once been in her grandfather's workshop. Smiling at her grandmother, she said, "Maybe later."

Louise moved to stand beside her. "This old thing brings back such memories."

A stab of remorse cut through Glory for having once suggested they sell it, and she placed her hand on the old stove. "I don't think we should put a price tag on it after all. Maybe we can make it a focal point of the shop. Give the place an old general store feel, with a fire glowing in it in the winter and chairs nearby for customers to stop in to chat and put their feet up."

Her grandmother patted her shoulder. "And I'll bet you think a barrel of pickles would top it off perfectly."

"Or not," Glory said, laughing at the silliness.

Pulling up a chair that needed to be stripped of old paint and stained, Louise settled on it and looked up at Glory with a light of expectation in her eyes. "It's all going to come together, just you watch. You have what it takes to make a go of it. You always have."

Glory felt a warm glow at her grandmother's praise, and leaned down to put her arms around her shoulders. "Thank you, Gram."

"I can hardly wait to see who your first client will be."

"*Our* first client," Glory corrected. But she wasn't ready to mention that she already had a job lined up. Not until she was in the house and doing the work, just to be on the safe side. After all, if it hadn't been for her grandmother's building that had stood empty for several years, they wouldn't even be talking about clients.

They both turned when the tiny bell above the door announced a visitor. "Why, hello," Louise greeted, while giving Glory a questioning glance.

But Glory was too surprised to say anything.

"Afternoon, Miz Gardner," the visitor said, nodding briefly at Glory's grandmother as he touched the brim of his black cowboy hat.

"Why, Dylan Walker, I haven't see you around for a—"

"Yes, what a surprise," Glory said, effectively cutting off the chitchat she suspected her grandmother would launch into without any encouragement. After that would come the invitation to Sunday dinner, and she certainly didn't want to go there. "Why don't we step into the office?"

But Louise didn't seem to hear. "Dylan, are you thinking of letting Glory work her magic on that wonderful old house of yours?"

Glory quickly spoke before he had a chance to answer her grandmother. "If you'll just come with me, Dylan…"

He looked from one woman to the other, his attention finally settling on Glory. "I just have a couple of questions."

"I really think we'll be more comfortable in my office," she tried again. After a brief hesitation, he followed her. "You'll have to excuse everything. We haven't had a chance to do much with the building. In fact, we aren't officially open yet."

He removed his hat, revealing his dark hair, and continued to stand. "Nice desk."

It took a moment for her to realize what he'd said. "It was my grandfather's."

"I thought so." He turned and pointed to the door. "That old wood burner out there, too?"

"Why, yes." She knew she shouldn't be surprised that he remembered one or the other. Her grandfather's leather shop had been famous for miles in every direction. The workshop, where he'd done the leather work, still stood behind the building. It had been her favorite place to visit when she could escape from the pressures at home, but Gramps had been gone for many years, and she'd barely been able to step inside his workshop since he'd died.

"It's nice of you to remember, Dylan. He had to give up the leather shop when the palsy got too bad to work."

Dylan placed his hat on the desk. "Erin's first saddle was one he'd made. I still remember how perfect the tooling was on it."

"Gram still has many of the things he made." And so had she, but she'd sold the last of them—her saddle—to Dylan's sister to get the money needed to pay the back taxes on the building so her grandmother wouldn't lose it.

Pushing the old memories deeper into her mind, she took a seat behind the desk and folded her hands on top of it. "What can I do for you, Dylan?"

"Like I said, I have a couple of questions."

Determined to be pleasant, she smiled and dipped her head in a nod. "Of course."

He continued to look at her, long and hard, making her skin prickle. "What experience do you have to complete this job my sister hired you for?"

It was her turn to stare. "I have a degree in art, if that's what you mean."

It was clear by his frown that he hadn't expected that kind of answer, but it didn't stop him. "Did my sister give you any instructions as to what to do if I refused to let you do any work on my house?"

Now she was in familiar territory. "As a matter of fact, she did warn me that you might not be receptive to having me there. As far as I'm concerned, it doesn't matter if you're there or not or whether you even want me there. I've been hired to do a job, and I intend to do it."

He was silent for a moment, as if thinking about what she'd said. "When do you plan to start?"

Now they were getting somewhere. "As soon as possible." His frown deepened, but she continued. "There won't be any real work at first. I'll need to take a look at the house and all the rooms, and take measurements of them. If you have specific ideas—"

"I don't. This wasn't my idea."

There was nothing she could say that would change things, so she didn't reply.

"How long will that take?" he asked.

She tried to quickly calculate the time and came up with a figure. "An hour, maybe an hour and a half, for the walk-through. Ballpark, of course. I'll have a better idea of how long the real work will take after that, but I suspect it will take at least a month, probably two."

He nodded, and she hoped the squint of his eyes and twist of his mouth was an indication that he was giving it all some thought. But there was no way of telling. She didn't know him well enough.

"Then you don't need me around for anything, right?"

The air in the room seemed much stuffier than when they'd first walked into the office, and she wished there had been a window to open. She'd also noticed that her heartbeat had kicked up a notch, the moment he'd stepped inside the shop, and it hadn't let up yet.

"If you don't want to be involved in the decisions, I can't force you to." She wasn't crazy about the idea of redecorating a house when the person who lived in it didn't have some kind of input, but it appeared that was the way it was going to be. She'd just have to hope that when she finished the job, he wouldn't hate it.

"Fair enough."

"So I have your permission to start?"

"Let's say I won't keep you from doing the job my sister hired you to do. How's that?"

It wasn't great, but it would do. "That's all I need. I'll start tomorrow morning."

She pushed away from the desk and stood. He followed suit, and she realized that to seal this business agreement—or the possibility of it, anyway—he would expect to shake on it. With a temerity she didn't feel, she stuck out her hand. She could have sworn that she saw one of his heavy, dark eyebrows lift just the slightest over his gorgeous green eyes, but he didn't hesitate when he took her hand in his.

They stood there for what seemed like an eternity, the warmth of his grasp making her slightly dizzy. She was certain it wasn't more than a second before he moved, yet didn't release her hand.

With his other hand, he reached into his shirt pocket and pulled something from it. He placed it on the desk, and she recognized her business card. "Interesting," he said.

Completely lost in his green eyes, all she could say was a nearly incoherent "What?"

"The card," he answered. "The Glory Be part."

Her mind was working in slow motion. "Oh. Yes. Well, it was…catchy."

Finally, he released her hand, picked up the card and returned it to his pocket. "Just in case."

"Y-yes. Just in case."

She watched as he replaced his hat, touched the brim of it with his index finger and turned to open the door and walk out of the office.

She was thankful her chair was available when her knees gave way.

DYLAN DIDN'T INTEND to notice the time as he parked the utility tractor next to his brother's barn. But when he did, his first thought was to wonder if Glory had started what she'd called her walk-through.

He wasn't completely convinced that he should have given her the okay to start working, but he really hadn't been given a choice. Erin had made sure of that. Did he really want Glory traipsing through his house when he wasn't there? Not that he thought she'd take anything or snoop around. But the idea of her being there alone just didn't sit well with him. Maybe he should check on her, just in case. At least if Erin called, he could tell her what was going on, and that should keep her off his case.

After shutting off the tractor, he climbed down and headed for his pickup.

"You're leaving already?" his brother called to him. "Hayley's stopping by with one of Kate McPherson's coffee cakes."

Dylan shook his head and opened the door of the truck. "Can't. I've got to get…" He needed an excuse. "I have an appointment I need to get to."

He was just sliding behind the wheel when Luke appeared at the door and closed it. "What kind of appointment? Are you sick?"

"Nah, nothing like that. Just…" He wasn't quite sure what or how much to tell his brother, so instead, he answered with, "I'll tell you about it later."

Luke stepped away from the truck as Dylan turned the key and started the engine. "You're sure you're all right?" Luke asked.

"Positive," he answered, knowing how much worry he'd caused his brother over the years.

"Okay." But Luke didn't look completely convinced.

With a quick nod, Dylan put the truck in gear and pulled out onto the road. During the short drive, he tried to think of how he might be able to get out of this crazy decorating deal his sister had dreamed up, but he knew the effort was useless. He knew Erin well enough to know that she wasn't going to let this go. And maybe she was right. Maybe he needed this. Maybe they all did. But that didn't mean he had to like it.

Turning into the long lane at his house, the first thing he noticed was the late-model sedan parked in front. With Glory nowhere in sight, he guessed she'd already gone inside. Climbing out of his truck, he headed for the enclosed porch, where he opened the wooden screen and stepped inside. For a moment, he hesitated, while his memories played their usual trick on him. His mother had had a green thumb, and the porch had always been filled with plants and flowers, often hiding the muddy boots and well-worn jackets and coats. The greenery was gone now, but it always took him a moment to accept it.

At the door that led from the porch to the kitchen, he noticed how badly it needed a coat of paint, much like everything else around the house. Since the death of his parents in a car accident, fifteen years before, he and his brother had focused on making the ranch the best they could, believing that was what their mom and dad would have wanted. But he'd ignored the house. Erin was right. It needed some work.

Opening the door, he stepped into the kitchen and stopped. Glory stood at the kitchen table with a camera in her hand, while she made notes on the papers in front of her.

She greeted him with a smile and put her pen on the table. "I hope it was all right that I let myself in. I looked around for you, and knocked on the door several times, but when no one answered…" She finished with a shrug.

He felt the first embers of anger, but quickly put them out. What did he expect her to do when he wasn't around? "I forgot you were going to be here," he said, but it was a lie.

"This house is amazing," she said, taking a step back away from the table and looking around the room.

In that briefest of moments, he saw the place through the eyes of a stranger. Embarrassed that he'd let things go so much, he wasn't sure what to say. "The folks weren't into fixing things up fancy."

"No, it isn't that. It's just… Well, to begin with, I haven't seen wallpaper like this for, oh, I don't know how long."

He took in the pattern of green ivy on the wall, and then the rest of the room. None of the appliances were anywhere near new. There was nothing as fancy as a dishwasher, and a large chest freezer took up most of one wall. But he'd never cared before, so why should he now?

"This table and chairs," she said with a sigh, from behind him.

He turned to look at the old chrome-and-vinyl kitchen set where his family had eaten every meal. "Yeah, it probably needs to be thrown out."

"Not necessarily," she said, but she frowned. "They're definitely retro, and people are looking for this type of thing. I wish they were in better condition."

He immediately stiffened at the slight. "The wallpaper's going, too, I suppose."

"Yes, I'm afraid so." Looking up, she smiled at him again. "Don't look so worried," she said, reaching out to put her hand on his arm. "I know what I'm doing."

He stared at her hand as the warmth of her touch snaked up his arm. Opening his mouth to tell her that she had no idea what she was doing to him, he immediately shut it again. He wasn't sixteen years old, and he had better sense than to let that perfume she was wearing—or her touch—get to him.

He cleared his throat as she pulled her hand away. "What about the appliances?" he asked. "Do I keep those?"

"That will depend on how much you want to upgrade."

Money hadn't been a problem for him and his brother for several years. They'd made out better than they'd ever thought they would. But he wanted this decorating thing to be over with as soon as possible.

Before he could come up with an answer, she continued. "We can discuss what might work well when we get further into this. As soon as I finish with measurements and a few more pictures, I'll start working on some ideas."

He hadn't expected it to be so easy. Maybe that meant it would be over quickly. "Okay. Sure."

She gathered her papers together and hooked her big bag over her shoulder. "I've always loved this house."

Having no memory of her coming to the Walker ranch, he looked at her to see if she was joking. She wasn't. "I guess I don't remember."

"It was a long time ago, but I've been here." She looked out the window where a row of trees lined the lane and continued on to the outbuildings. "When we were in eighth grade, both classes came out here for a hayride." She turned to look at him. "Don't you remember?"

He couldn't even drag up a foggy memory of it. That didn't surprise him. He'd blocked so many things from his childhood, after the accident. "Sorry, no, I don't."

"Oh."

"There's a lot I don't remember. After—" He shook his head, unable to continue.

"Now I'm the one who's sorry."

"No reason you should be." They stood in an uncomfortable silence, until he finally broke it. "When do you think you'll be finished?"

"With the job?" she asked. "That depends on how much you want done."

It didn't matter to him, as long as it satisfied his sister and he was left alone. "Whatever you and Erin talked about."

"A couple of months. Maybe more."

He didn't like the sound of it. "That long?"

She looked around, as if trying to get her bearings. "I could hire some extra help."

"That's okay. Whatever it takes." She didn't seem to

understand that it wasn't him she had to please but his sister. Even if he was the one who was paying for it.

Her head bobbed in a nod. "I'll just get those measurements...."

When she'd gathered her things and walked into the dining room, he blew out a long breath. He only hoped he wouldn't be running into her every time he turned around. The sooner she could get the job done, the better. And then his life would get back to normal. Quiet, uninterrupted and without Glory Andrews in it.

Chapter Two

Even before the sun had slipped into the sky the next morning, Glory was out of bed and eager to start work. Anticipation rippled through her as she drove out of town, headed for the Walker ranch and her first job. She was finally coming into her own, ready to prove her worth, not only in the decorating world, but in life. It was past time, and she was excited.

She was less than two miles from the ranch when doubts started tiptoeing into her thoughts. When he stopped in the shop the day before, Dylan hadn't been any more eager than when she'd first told him his sister had hired her. Having no idea what he did or didn't like could be disastrous, and guessing wasn't necessarily a good thing. She didn't know his tastes in types of furniture or even his favorite color. If she knew him better… But she didn't, and she hadn't gotten the impression that he was going to be forthcoming with any information.

Glancing next to her at the stack of binders and the large portfolio containing photos and sketches that would provide the inspiration needed, she took a deep breath.

"I can do this," she announced in the silence of the car. It helped a little and as she slowed to turn into the long lane that led to the Walker house, she felt a familiar confidence wash over her. Yes, she could do this.

After climbing out of the car, Glory looked around and spied what she guessed was Dylan's truck near the big barn in the distance. Although she felt fairly certain he wouldn't be any more pleasant than he had been the day before, she walked in that direction so she could let him know she'd arrived.

Determined to remain positive and friendly, she stepped out of the sunshine and through the large open doors at one end of the barn. Once inside, she waited until her eyes adjusted to the dim interior of the cavernous building.

"Oh, there you are," she said when she spotted him. "You know, this barn looks even bigger from the inside. Was it built about the same time as the house?"

He didn't bother to do more than glance at her. "Yeah, it's one of the oldest barns in the area that's still standing."

"Things were built well back then. Not so much now," she said, sighing. "We've made everything disposable. I'll take the old over the new." She felt him watching her, but he said nothing. Somehow she needed to discover what he might like her to do with his house. After all, that was why she was there—not to make conversation.

"I was thinking I wouldn't do as much work upstairs," she continued. "Maybe just freshen the paint and some other basic things." When he didn't comment, she hurried on to add, "But if you'd like more done—"

"None of those rooms have been used since Luke built the new house for Kendra."

Having learned from her grandmother that his brother's marriage had ended abruptly, two years earlier, leaving Luke with a baby son to raise, she understood the hint of animosity in Dylan's voice. She also knew Luke and his new fiancée were in the wedding-planning stage, but Dylan didn't seem willing to say more.

Ignoring the awkward moment, she took a step back, ready to get to work. "I'll go on up to the house, then."

"It's unlocked."

Smiling, she nodded. "Yes, I don't doubt it. Only here in the rural areas do people leave their houses unlocked. In the city, that's an open invitation to thieves."

When he didn't respond, she gave a small wave and turned to leave. Once she was outside, she breathed a sigh of relief and hurried to her car, where she unloaded the things she'd need for the day.

She chose to work in the dining room, hoping that doing so would keep her out of Dylan's way. Unpacking, she sorted and stacked her material on the long dining table. Then she opened the door into an enclosed stairwell and climbed the stairs to the second floor. Her notes from the day before were hastily scribbled, and she double-checked the measurements of the upstairs rooms.

When she returned to the dining room, she found Dylan standing near the table, her drawings from the folders in his hands.

He looked up as she came farther into the room. "Is this what you're going to do?"

She wasn't sure if he'd understand that they were simple sketches. "Yes and no," she said, watching his face as he studied the pictures.

"You could do this?" He pointed to a photo of a kitchen she'd found.

Still unsure, she gave a small nod. "Something similar, yes. Do you like it?"

He shrugged and replaced the papers and pictures on the table. "It's okay."

"Those are just ideas," she hurried to say. "I hadn't really decided on anything, so if you don't like—"

"Never said I didn't."

The deep timbre of his voice took her breath away, and she ignored it. At least she now had an idea of what he might like to see in the way of changes. Unable to stop her smile, she let her enthusiasm carry her away. "I have more pictures and ideas for the other rooms. Do you want to see them? We can go over them, and you can choose the ones you like."

He shook his head and shoved away from the wall. "No reason to do that."

Her smile died along with her excitement, while a sinking feeling replaced her enthusiasm. Gathering some papers in the hopes of appearing more professional than she felt at that moment, she searched for something to say, with no luck.

"Look," he said, "I wouldn't be doing this if—" He lowered his head, shaking it.

Glory thought of what Erin had told her about Dylan still having a hard time with the memory of losing their mom and dad. She couldn't blame him. She could still remember when it happened, a few weeks before graduation. Dylan had looked so sad and lost as he'd walked across the stage of the high school to accept his diploma. Like many others, she'd had tears in her eyes and reminded herself that, no matter how hard things sometimes were for her at home, it was nothing like what he was going through.

"Yes, okay," she said. "I'll do my best."

"So you think you can do it? In two months?"

Her spirits lifted. "I'm sure I can. You won't even recognize the place when I'm done." Her mind raced with ideas. "I'll work on a few more sketches and make a list of supplies I'll need to have delivered. There will be a lot of changes, and they won't be quick. New cabinets and counters in the kitchen—"

"Whatever works."

Her heart sank again, and she tried to gather her wits. He didn't care or at least he pretended not to, and she needed to accept that. This wasn't the way she had imagined her first decorating job would be, but she'd find a way to do it, whether he was involved or not. She needed to be a success, and this was her chance.

"Just how much am I paying you for this?" he asked, breaking into her thoughts. When she named a figure she'd roughed out, his dark, heavy eyebrows drew together over his green eyes. "That much?"

Panic hit, but she squared her shoulders. His sister had assured her that she'd be well paid, no matter what he said or did. Lifting her chin with all the pride and determination she could gather, she said, "If you think it's too much, maybe we should—"

"Is it?"

For a moment, she was totally taken aback. "No," she said. "No, it isn't. Certainly not in today's market."

"Will you be here tomorrow?"

"First thing in the morning," she said. "If that's all right."

He looked away. "Whatever works for you. I don't care."

When he didn't say more, she took a step back. "I don't know exactly what time I'll be here."

"It's always unlocked." Without saying anything else, he disappeared into the kitchen.

She heard the sound of his boots on the floor and the screen door closing. Although she was a little shaken, she decided she'd handled their little encounter fairly well. She would have to get used to the fact that he obviously didn't have much to say, unless he thought it was important. That was all right with her. She didn't need the distraction. Getting involved with someone again was the last thing on her mind, no matter how green his eyes were.

Later, when she'd finished looking over each of the rooms again and making copious notes she probably wouldn't use, she climbed into her car and drove away. When she pulled out onto the paved road, headed for town, she took her cell phone from her purse and hit an autodial button. "Erin?" she said when a young woman answered. "I wanted to let you know that I've begun work on the house."

"Wonderful!" Dylan's sister replied. "I know you'll do a terrific job and I can't wait to visit the first chance I get. Is he cooperating?"

Glory wasn't quite sure how to answer. "Well, he didn't throw me out."

Erin laughed, and they talked for a few more minutes about what Glory planned to do. When the call was over, she hoped Dylan would be happy with the changes, too. But it was hard to tell much of anything about him.

"WHO'S THAT?" LUKE ASKED.

Standing in the opening of the big barn, Dylan looked out to see Glory's car coming up the lane. Before he could answer, a pickup with Mercer's Hardware painted on the door turned into the lane behind it.

Luke took a step outside. "So you're really going to do some work on the house?"

Turning to his brother, Dylan shrugged. "I told you that Erin said I needed to do something. Renovate, fix it up, whatever."

"Well, yeah, but I didn't know that meant you were going to go through with it." Luke was silent for a moment as they both watched the vehicles come to a stop near the screened-in porch. "Wait a second," he said when Glory climbed out of her car and walked over to the pickup. "She doesn't work at Mercer's."

"No, she—"

"Hey, that's Glory Caldwell."

"Andrews."

Luke turned to him. "What?"

"Used to be Caldwell. She married Kyle Andrews."

"Oh, yeah," Luke said, turning back to watch what was going on. "So they're back in town?"

"I guess." But Dylan didn't know for sure. She still hadn't mentioned anything about her husband. Not that there was any reason to.

"You'd think we would have heard they were back. From what I remember of Kyle, he wasn't shy about tooting his own horn."

"Yeah, that was Kyle." But Dylan hadn't been surprised when Glory married the guy. After all, she was the Prom Queen and Kyle had been the King. Everybody said they belonged together. Dylan hadn't questioned that. He'd just watched her from afar, like all the other guys had. Watching was all he'd done. There'd been no foolish ideas about asking her out. He'd known better, even then.

"Why is she here?"

Dylan wasn't real happy about having to answer the question, but he couldn't ignore it, so he hedged. "She has a decorating business."

Luke looked at him. "Yeah?"

"Yeah."

"In Desperation?"

Dylan was getting tired of answering questions. "Yeah, in that building her grandmother still owns. The one with her grandfather's workshop in the back."

"And she's doing the decorating stuff here, at your house?"

Not that he wanted to, but Dylan nodded.

Glory had walked around to the back of the pickup with the driver, who was unloading several gallons of paint, along with some boxes. While the driver took the buckets toward the house, she walked in the opposite direction, stopped and lifted her hand to her eyes. She was looking for him.

Dylan had planned to be absent when she arrived. In fact, he'd decided it might be best to stay clear of her as much as possible, considering that he never felt quite like himself when she was around. But when he saw her wave, there wasn't a whole lot he could do.

"Go on," Luke said. "I'll meet you at the house in a minute. I need to fill my water jug."

"Why should I?"

On his way to grab his jug from the back of his pickup, Luke stopped and looked back. "Because she probably needs to talk to you."

"No, she doesn't."

Luke didn't move. "It's your house."

"Right."

"You make the decisions about what happens with it."

Dylan knew he should agree, but then he would have to explain about their sister and how she'd managed to hornswoggle him into agreeing to let someone—who turned out to be Glory—work on his house.

"Like I said, it was Erin's idea to make some changes," he said, ending the discussion.

It was obvious that he wasn't going to be able to avoid Glory. As he walked toward where she stood, he saw her say something to the driver, who then got in the pickup and drove away.

"I didn't mean to take you away from your work," she said when he drew closer to the house.

Wishing his brother had been anyplace else besides next to him at the barn when Glory pulled in, he spied the paint and boxes by the door to the porch. "Need a hand getting this stuff inside?"

"Oh! Yes, I guess I could use a little help. Thank you for noticing."

He loaded his hands and arms with paint cans, and she hurried to open the door for him. "Where do you want them?" he asked, carrying them into the house.

"Here in the kitchen is fine."

He set them down by the door, and then stood there, wondering how to get out of this uncomfortable situation he was now in. He'd never spent a lot of time talking to women, except for the occasional "howdy, ma'am" or to answer a question about his health, which was always good. Not that he'd been celibate. There were ways. But standing in the kitchen with nothing to say while Glory looked around the room from top to bottom was proof that he wasn't at the head of the class when it came to his conversational skills.

He watched as she walked across the room and stopped at the doorway that led to his bedroom. Not that he particularly needed to watch, but he couldn't help it. There was something in the way she moved, but he managed to turn his attention away from her. After all, she was a married woman. She and Kyle had been together for forever.

"Have you ever considered using this for a ranch office?" she asked, looking over her shoulder at him.

"No, I never have." He tended to do paperwork at the kitchen table and store that same paperwork in a corner in his bedroom or the dining room. He'd always thought it was foolish for him to have the house, but that was the way it had worked out. Once Luke turned eighteen and graduated from high school, Erin left for the rodeo circuit and rarely came home. He and his brother had shared the house. When Luke decided to marry Kendra, she'd vetoed the idea that Dylan would move out and let them have the house. Instead, she'd insisted on a big, new house, and Luke had had it built.

Glory's eyes shone. "I have some great ideas for it."

"For what?"

"For an office. It would be perfect."

"So I guess I'll sleep upstairs, then," he said, thinking aloud and not realizing he'd actually spoken.

Nodding, she faced him and asked, "Which room do you think you'd like?"

Before he could tell her that none of them would suit him, he heard the screen door on the porch open and close. He could almost taste the relief when Luke stepped into the kitchen.

"I hope I'm not interrupting anything," Luke said, looking from Glory to Dylan.

"Nope," Dylan answered, ready to escape the house.

"We were just discussing the idea of making an office in here for ranch business." She pointed to the room behind her. Her smile grew and she laughed, shaking her head. "I can't believe I'm standing here in this house with the Walker brothers."

"It's good to see you, Glory," Luke said, glancing at Dylan. "I heard you've opened a new business in town."

"I have. Glory Be Antiques and Decorating. We aren't officially open yet, but when Erin and I ran into each other in Texas and she learned about my plans..." She shrugged and smiled at both of them.

"I remember your grandad's leather shop," Luke said. "There was nothing like it for hundreds of miles."

Glory's smile dimmed, and Dylan recognized the sadness in her eyes. "He loved making saddles," she said. "It broke his heart when he couldn't work anymore. And then he..." She took a breath. "But the shop is still there. I think Gram has been thinking of selling his tools. She's mentioned it. I'm not sure what we'll do with the space. I—" She lowered her head for a moment, and then raised it again, smiling. "Maybe I'll use it for a workroom myself. Someday. It's— Let's just say it's difficult for both of us to go in there without thinking of him."

Luke glanced at Dylan, and then nodded in agreement at Glory. "I understand completely. So you've moved back to town permanently?"

This time her smile was sincere. "I hope so. I've missed Desperation. And I hope we can make a success of the business."

"The town hasn't changed that much. And with Kyle's connections, you shouldn't have a problem getting customers."

Dylan, who'd been watching her throughout the conversation, noticed that her smile dimmed considerably when his brother mentioned her husband's name.

"Kyle and I have been divorced for some time," she said, avoiding eye contact with either of them.

Dylan was too surprised to hear what Luke was saying. Her announcement left him stunned, and he wondered just how big of a fool Kyle Andrews was to have let Glory Caldwell go. Not that it changed anything, he told himself. Whether she was married or not made no difference. She'd been hired to fix up his house. But in the back of his mind was the thought that he definitely needed to give her a wide berth. He'd already thought about her too many times, and it wasn't the kind of thing he should be doing.

"ARE YOU GOING to the Walker place today?" Louise asked.

Glory nodded. She placed her coffee cup on the kitchen table and rolled up the plans she'd worked on in the evenings during the past week. "The man who's tearing out the kitchen cabinets will be there in about fifteen minutes, so I need to get going."

"Is everything working out all right? I mean, with the Walker boy."

Glory turned to look at her grandmother and wondered how to answer. It wasn't Dylan's fault that she'd begun to form an unwanted attraction to him. She certainly couldn't tell her grandmother about that. Gram would be thrilled, she was sure. Dylan, not so much. He barely knew she was there. Which, she reminded herself, was as it should be.

"Dylan is a very nice man," she answered as she headed for the door. "He isn't crazy about me being there and doesn't care what I do to the house, but I have faith it will all work out."

"Oh."

Her grandmother's disappointment was so clear that Glory had to bite her cheek to keep from laughing, even though it wasn't funny. It would break Gram's heart to know she had absolutely no desire to form any kind of relationship with Dylan Walker or anyone else, no matter how often she thought of him and enjoyed getting glimpses of him throughout her day. After all, he was more than easy on the eyes. But she was determined to keep her mind on business, not on him.

"I'd better get going," she said, needing to escape her grandmother's questioning eyes. "I have some things I need to talk over with him before he gets busy with ranch work. I'll see you later."

After kissing her grandmother's cheek, she hurried out the door and to her car. A quick look at her watch told her she didn't have time to enjoy the drive, and she turned her mind to the work she needed to do that day.

When she arrived at the ranch, she immediately noticed that Dylan's pickup was parked near the barn. Her heartbeat picked up. She pressed her lips together and reminded herself that she was there on business. And business was all she was interested in. Focusing her thoughts on the job ahead, she decided that the things she needed to talk to him about could wait.

She'd just climbed out of her car when another pickup, this one pulling an empty trailer, turned into the long drive and parked behind her. "Good morning," she called to Jim White, who climbed out of the vehicle and approached her.

With a touch to the brim of his cap, he nodded. "Morning, Miz Andrews. The town's buzzin' with the news that you're back."

She felt the heat of a blush on her face, but smiled. "I hope it's a happy buzzing."

He followed her up to the house. "It is, for sure," he assured her. "Now what all is it you want me to do here?"

Ready to get to work, Glory led him into the kitchen and explained what needed to be done. Gathering the photos from the dining room, she showed them to him, so he'd have an idea of what she envisioned it would look like, once the old was gone and the new was finished.

"It's mighty nice," he answered. "Who's doin' your cabinetry?"

She understood that this was the way it was in small towns. In a big city, it didn't matter. A job was a job, and most people didn't know the other contractors, unless they'd worked with them before. "I heard good things about Ned Parker, so he's doing it."

He nodded. "I don't think he'll disappoint you."

"I have some things to get out of my car, and then I'll be working in the living room." She pointed to the doorway. "If you need me, I'll be in there."

"Yes'm," he replied, and began to lay out his tools.

Satisfied that she could leave him to his work, she returned to her car for a box. After spending the past week stripping wallpaper upstairs in what she had chosen to be the master bedroom, she'd done some research and come up with what she hoped would make the job in the living room go more quickly.

Closing the car door, she glanced toward the barn and, to her surprise, she caught sight of Dylan, standing in the doorway of the barn and looking her way. A second later, he was gone, and she wondered if he'd been watching her.

"Of course not," she scolded herself, under her breath. He wasn't interested in her, only her work, and barely that, considering how much she'd seen him since she'd started working on the house. "You're letting your imagination run away with you, and for no reason."

In the house again, she put thoughts of Dylan Walker as far away as possible and concentrated on dampening the old wallpaper with a mixture of water and vinegar, applied with a mister attached to an old canister vacuum she'd found. To her surprise, it helped, and she was busy spraying and stripping when, out of the corner of her eye, she noticed Dylan walk in.

"What's that smell?" he asked over the noise.

"Vinegar," she told him, turning off the vacuum. "It's supposed to help cut the wallpaper paste. They didn't make strippable paper back when this was hung."

"I guess it's been there for as long as I can remember."

There was a note of pure sadness in his voice, and she didn't know how to respond to it. Deciding it was probably best not to, she said instead, "While you're here..."

He ducked his head and stuffed his hands in the pockets of his jeans. "Yeah?"

His eyes had narrowed, but she'd quickly learned it meant nothing. "It would be a big help if I knew what furniture you want to keep and what to get rid of."

For a moment, she was frightened by the look on his face. It was so intense, she couldn't even put a name to it.

"Get rid of all of it," he said with a wave of his hand. Turning around, he strode to the door.

But Glory wasn't ready to let him walk out on such an announcement. She didn't know what she had said to upset him, but she couldn't just let him leave.

"Wait, Dylan," she said and hurried to catch him.

When she did, she placed her hand on his arm. "We need to talk about this."

He stopped and looked down at her hand on his arm. She immediately withdrew it. Turning to face her he asked, "What's there to talk about?"

Resolving not to let him intimidate her, she took a deep breath to calm her racing heart. "Most of the furniture is too good to simply throw away. Are you sure you don't want to keep it?"

"I don't need it, do I? Can't you just clear it all out and replace it with new furniture?"

She noticed that his jaw had tightened, and she sensed she needed to stay calm and explain. "Of course I can," she assured him. "But throwing it away is foolish. Many of these things might be old, but they're well made. Some could even be collector's items."

His eyes narrowed again, but this time it seemed more thoughtful than intimidating. "Like the antiques I saw in your shop?"

Relieved that he was beginning to understand, she nodded. "Some of them."

"So take them and sell them, if they'll make money for you."

She tried not to smile. "I think I have a better idea. Why don't I sell them on consignment? That way, we'd both benefit. That's what Gram and I agreed to do if people brought things in to sell."

"So you keep part of the money and I get the rest?"

She tried to ignore his frown. "Exactly."

"I don't need the money."

"Then give it to charity. It doesn't matter to me who gets it."

He seemed to consider the suggestion, but didn't say anything. When he started to walk away, she wasn't ready for him to leave yet. "Maybe we should go through things today. The more I can move out of here, the better."

"Not today."

He sounded so final that she nearly took a step back. "All right. What about tomorrow? I might be able to find a few high school boys to help load the furniture, if you and Luke could provide the pickups to haul it to my shop."

"Not tomorrow, either. I'll be in the city."

"Oh." She hoped she didn't sound as disappointed as she felt. Not that she had a reason to be.

"Hayley's getting her master's degree at OU Med Center tomorrow. And then there's some kind of party for her in town, after that."

Glory suddenly felt left out, but dismissed it, reminding herself that she'd been gone for too many years to simply pick up where she'd left off. "That's wonderful, Dylan. Please tell her congratulations for me."

Without saying anything else, he nodded and left the room. She remembered him being quiet in school, but not nearly so serious. If only she could see a glimpse of that boy he had been.

It didn't matter, she told herself, getting back to work. At least she'd have a couple of days to work on the house, without anyone around. She hated to admit it, even to herself, but she would miss seeing him, although he'd left no doubt that having her around was more of a nuisance than anything else—proof that she needed to keep her work and career uppermost in her mind. The question was whether she could.

Chapter Three

Dylan couldn't believe he'd let his brother talk him into staying late at the reception after Hayley's graduation. Even worse, what on earth had possessed him to let them drag him along afterward to a late dinner with a good twenty people he hadn't the least desire to talk to? The best part was that it was over, and he wouldn't have to deal with something like it again. Except Luke and Hayley's wedding, and there'd be no begging off of that.

As he turned into the drive leading to his house, he was surprised to see Glory's car still there. It was close to midnight, and he hoped she wasn't still working. Getting out of the car, he grunted his concern. He'd have to start paying her overtime.

Having her around had become an interesting experience. She hadn't been someone in school that a person could ignore, but he hadn't known her well. Not that he needed to. In fact, the less he saw of her, the better.

Ready to tell her in no uncertain terms to go home, he spied her before he stepped from the porch into the open kitchen doorway. Her head rested on a stack of what he guessed were books containing some kind of samples, while she slept soundly, oblivious to the fact that he was in the room.

He watched her, knowing he might seem a little like

a stalker, but he couldn't stop himself. Her lips were slightly parted, as if she had something she wanted to say, and a strand of hair had fallen across the slender bridge of her nose, while thick eyelashes rested on creamy skin. She looked like an angel. An imperfect one, but beautiful, all the same. He knew he shouldn't stand there and stare.

Looking up, he noticed the upper cabinets were missing. He couldn't imagine that the job would be done in two months. It seemed that the longer the remodeling went on, the worse it got. The kitchen was only one room. There was no telling what the rest of the house looked like.

Stepping as lightly as possible, he moved to his right and slipped into the dining room. Even that rarely used room was a mess. The curtains had been removed and the floor was covered in plastic. The heavy dining table and ten chairs were stacked in a corner, beneath more plastic. The wallpaper was mostly gone, and he wrinkled his nose at the smell of vinegar that filled the air.

In the living room, he found the same conditions, although it was hard to see in the dark. When he flipped the light switch, he discovered the lights weren't working. After taking a closer look, he saw that the fixtures were gone. Everything was chaos.

He turned to find Glory standing in the doorway to the kitchen, watching him. He didn't doubt that he looked angry. He'd never seen such a disaster in his life, and although something inside him didn't want to upset her with his quickly growing fury, he knew he'd failed by the fear on her face.

"I know it looks like it'll never be done, right now," she said, her voice husky with sleep.

"Yeah, it does" was all he could say. He watched as

she lifted her chin, but he didn't know if it was in pride or defiance. No matter which one it was, he couldn't tell her it was all right, because it wasn't.

"I promise it will be better." Her chest rose and fell as she took a deep breath. "It really will. It'll only be like this for a few days."

He winced at the thought of dealing with the mess for much longer. "How many?"

"Well…" She glanced around the room before offering him a weak smile. "The kitchen will probably be the last to be finished."

"When?"

"Two or three weeks. Maybe four?"

He tried not to let her see how disappointed he was and how angry that made him. He usually had more control, but with Glory, he was learning that control wasn't always so easy. "I guess it's too late to change my mind."

He hadn't meant for it to sound the way it had come out of his mouth. He'd been half joking. Before he could take it back or explain, she turned and disappeared down the hall. "Glory," he called, but all he heard was her footsteps on the wood floor.

A moment later, she answered. "It really will be better soon."

Relief swept through him, but he wasn't sure why. "Okay, I believe you." Did he have a choice?

She reappeared in the dining room doorway, having obviously circled around through the kitchen. "Thanks for trying."

"I'm not—"

"Yes, you are." She smiled. "It's all right. I really do understand that it seems like the work will never get done," she said, waving her arm to encompass the whole house. "But if you'll just be patient—"

"It's not—"

"Don't say it, please," she begged.

He wasn't the kind of man who enjoyed hurting someone, and he wouldn't make her the exception. "It was a shock to see it, that's all," he explained when she came into the room. "I'm sure you'll make it right."

She settled on what he suspected was the large sofa, hidden beneath a white sheet. "You *hope* it will be all right."

"Do I have a choice?"

She leaned her head back against the sofa and laughed. "No, I suppose you don't, although it's always a possibility." Closing her eyes, she sighed and smiled. "Tell me what it was like growing up here in this house."

Her request surprised him, and he wasn't sure how to answer. He also wasn't sure he wanted to take a trip back to a past he'd spent fifteen years trying not to think about. "There's not much to tell."

She turned her head and looked at him with wide eyes. "I don't believe you."

His answer was a shrug. The way she sat studying him was causing his body to react in ways it shouldn't have, and he looked away.

"I know you all worked hard. That's always a given on a farm or a ranch. And you know it wasn't like that for me. But that's not what I'm asking about."

In the silence that followed, he knew she was waiting for him to say something. "I don't know what you mean."

"Okay." He heard her take a deep breath. "What's your best memory of growing up?"

"I don't know. I don't think I have any."

"Oh, surely you do!"

He was forced to look at her. "No, really. I don't remember much."

She shook her head, her disbelief achingly clear. "All right. I understand that you don't want to share with me."

"It's not that I don't want to. I just—"

"It's all right, Dylan," she said, straightening her shoulders and lifting her chin. "I have my own memories."

She'd grabbed his curiosity, so when she started to stand, he couldn't let her leave it at that. "Like what?"

"Like that hayride you don't remember. All the times Tracy— You remember Tracy Billings? She was my best friend. When we weren't riding horses at her place in the summer, we were hiding under the bleachers at the park to watch you at Little League practice."

"You're kidding," he said, sure they'd done no such thing.

"Not at all."

"Someone would have seen you."

Her smile was impish. "You have no idea how sneaky little girls can be when they want to watch little boys they have crushes on."

"Crushes?" Now she'd snagged his attention and he wanted to hear more. Had he really been one of those crushes?

With an odd smile, she gave him a dismissive wave of her hand and looked away. "Lots of them. A new one every summer. Sometimes." She turned back toward him. "Baseball was important to you, wasn't it?"

"More important than breathing." He'd won an athletic scholarship to college, but he hadn't taken it. After his parents' accident, he felt he had to stay and help keep the ranch running. Luke had still been in high school, and Erin had offered to stay and help.

"Those were some of the best times of my life," she said. "Those times with Tracy when we were kids."

He was surprised to hear the sadness in her voice, but didn't ask why. It wasn't any of his business.

"If it's all right," she said, standing, "I'll straighten up a little and go home. I'm tired." She walked toward the kitchen, then stopped and looked back at him. "I promise it will get better. Okay?"

He nodded and she disappeared, leaving him with questions and a tiny hole in the wall he'd built around his memories for the past fifteen years. He wondered if she had any idea what that meant to him. He'd forgotten how happy his childhood had been. He just wasn't sure yet if that was good or bad and hoped he wouldn't regret it when he learned which one.

GLORY'S SIGH ECHOED in the upstairs hallways. Once again, she'd forgotten something. This time it was the faceplates for the wall switches. The electrician would arrive soon to put the new light fixtures in the bedrooms, and she'd wanted everything to be ready. Now she'd have to make a trip into town.

"Hey, Miz Andrews?"

She smiled at the luck she'd had in hiring three high school boys to help out. It hadn't hurt that one of them had grown up helping his mother wallpaper, and that another was a wizard with a paintbrush.

As she started down the stairs, she spied the tall, dark-haired young man waiting at the bottom. "What is it, Mark?"

"Stu said he'd be here a little late. He promised his mom he'd go with her to the farmer's market this morning, now that school is out. He said to tell you he'll stay late, if you need him."

She stopped two steps from the bottom of the stairs and looked directly at Mark. A blush crept up his face, and he looked down as she spoke. "I don't see why he'll need to stay late. And you're here awfully early, aren't you?"

"Yes, ma'am," he answered, still refusing to meet her gaze. "I woke up early and thought I'd give you a hand with whatever needed to get done this morning before Brent gets here."

"I really appreciate that, Mark. The electrician should be arriving anytime, so I'm glad you'll be here when he does. I need to run into town for the faceplates, and Mr. Walker seems to have been an early riser, too."

"No problem."

She smiled. The boys were eager to help, and she counted herself very lucky to have them. Dylan had made himself scarce since their little bit of reminiscing on Saturday night. No matter how early she arrived, he was gone, and she suspected he was avoiding her. It was just as well. She needed to focus on the job, not him. Even so, it would be wise to let him know she was leaving, just in case someone needed her.

She took the last two steps. "I'll let Mr. Walker know I'm leaving."

Mark nodded and moved out of the way as she walked to the kitchen. Grabbing her bag, she looped it over her shoulder and went outside, heading for the barn.

It was a beautiful morning, with only a hint of a breeze stirring the leaves on the trees. Dew glittered in the sunshine, and the scent of flowers drifted around her. There was so much she loved about her hometown and the surrounding countryside. In spite of her failed marriage, she'd enjoyed living in North Carolina and marveled at the beauty of Charlotte. But Desperation, Oklahoma, would always be home to her.

As she walked closer to the barn, she spotted Dylan's pickup parked on the far side. At least she'd been right, she thought, as she climbed through the corral fence. Moving to the oversize opening of the big barn, she waited for her eyes to adjust, and then looked around for Dylan.

If she hadn't seen movement out of the corner of her eye, she might have missed him as he worked along the back wall of the barn. "There you are," she called to him.

He stopped and looked in her direction. "What are you doing out here? You'll get dirty."

"Like when I'm in the house stripping wallpaper and sanding?"

"Worse. That's nothing but dried paste and some dust. This is—"

"Mud and manure? I can live with that."

He didn't answer right away. "Was there something you wanted?"

What she really wanted was for him to relax around her—it would make her work a lot more pleasant. But he'd become even more guarded than before. If only she could get a glimpse of the boy he'd once been—the one whose rare smile had been the reason she and her friends had gone to the baseball games. But she sensed that if she told him, he wouldn't believe her.

Swallowing a sigh, she answered his question. "I wanted to let you know that I'm going into town. Is there anything you need that I can bring back?"

"Not that I know of." He turned away from whatever he was doing and faced her. "I see you found some helpers. How are they working out?"

"They're perfect," she answered, and then thought of something. "You didn't have anything to do with them applying for the job, did you?"

"Nope. Didn't need to. You never had a problem getting guys to help you."

For a brief moment, she thought of telling him that he was wrong, but he wasn't. She'd been blessed with a special talent for enlisting whatever help she needed.

"I suppose you're right," she finally answered. "But I don't do it on purpose."

"Never said you did. Just be careful."

"Careful? Of what?"

"They're boys. And you're... Well, you're Glory."

She opened her mouth to ask what he meant, but before she could, he'd disappeared. Turning for the big barn door, she wondered exactly what it was he remembered about her. For someone she'd barely known, even though they'd gone all through school together, he seemed to know her fairly well. Or thought he did. Had talking about the past, three nights before, been a mistake? If it had been, she was sorry. She hadn't meant to make him uncomfortable. Maybe she should try to be more aware of his feelings, but that would require him showing some, and she wasn't sure how to break through that wall he'd built around himself. And there was really no reason to try. Besides, she finally felt good about herself, and not because of what others thought. Why mess up a good thing?

The trip to town was quick, thanks to finding exactly what she wanted at the hardware store, and she was back at the ranch minutes before the electrician arrived. With the help of Mark and Brent, the boxes containing the light fixtures were soon upstairs in the circular hallway.

"The chandelier goes in there." Glory pointed to the room at the top of the stairs. She was the only person who'd been in it since she'd finished the painting and papering, but this was the day she planned to unveil Dylan's new bedroom to him. Once everything was done, anyway.

"This one first, then?" the electrician asked.

Being both eager and apprehensive about the outcome of this first and most important room, she hesitated. Considering how Dylan had refused to give her any input— "Yes, do it first," she said.

Maybe forcing him to acknowledge her work in a positive way would bring him around. It was worth a try. How much more could he avoid her, without completely disappearing or firing her? Before she panicked that he might, she reminded herself that Erin wouldn't let that happen. Since Dylan wasn't cooperating, she'd been in touch with his sister about everything that was done or that she planned to do. Erin was fine with all of it.

After taking a deep breath, she followed the boys into the room to see their reaction to the work she'd done.

"Wow," Brent whispered to Mark, only a foot away from her.

"Yeah," Mark answered, his eyebrows raised and his eyes wide as he looked around the room.

Glory wondered if that was a bad *wow* or a good one, but the electrician was giving instructions to the boys, so she couldn't ask.

"Hold it steady," the electrician ordered as he perched high on the ladder. "These nosebleed ceilings are enough to make a grown man think twice about a lot of things."

"That's the charm of old houses," she said, without thinking.

The man on the ladder looked down at her, a frown pulling at his mouth. "You wouldn't think so if you'd had to deal with the nightmare wiring that I have. Luckily, it's been kept fairly updated here."

"That's good," she answered. "I hope the plumbing is the same. I'm thinking of updating the bath up here."

As soon as it was out of her mouth, she wondered where it had come from. She'd had no intention of doing anything more than redecorating upstairs. But now that the idea had surfaced, it wasn't such a bad one. She'd run it by Erin first, though.

"Who would you recommend for that kind of thing?" she asked.

"Hand me that rope, there, boys," he called down to them. "Well, now, Miz Andrews, there's a couple of plumbers in the area, although not all of them from Desperation."

As he named off several people, she wished she had a paper and pencil on her. "Maybe I should just try—"

Certain she heard a noise on the stairs, she hurried to the door and into the hall. Dylan stood at the top of the stairs, one hand on the railing.

"Doesn't anybody hear me?" he asked. "And what the devil are you doing in there?"

The last thing Glory wanted was for him to see the room before it was completely finished. Considering the string of words coming from the electrician at that moment, she had a feeling it might not be soon.

"Just having a new light fixture hung," she said, joining him. "Is there something you need?"

"Yeah—you."

Her breath caught and she stared at him. She felt

warm, deep inside, and immediately scolded herself. If she had any sense, she'd turn around and run—

"I need you to go downstairs," he was saying, his dark brows drawn together in a frown. "There's some guy delivering something. I'm guessing it's the kitchen cabinets. I need his truck out of the way, but he says he can't move it until he's unloaded it."

It took a few seconds for her mind to wrap around what was happening, and when she did, she felt like a fool. "Of course," she said, still a bit unsteady and hoping her voice didn't wobble. "Let me get Mark and Brent. We'll have the truck unloaded immediately."

"Good." He turned and bounded down the stairs, leaving her to wish she could find a way to stop the lustful thoughts she was having about him. He wasn't interested in her. It wasn't as though she wanted him to be. As if he ever would. Except for a few rare times, he'd been cold and unreachable—the last things she found sexy in a man.

But as she called to the boys to come help, it took more concentration than it should have to put a stop to those lustful thoughts.

FROM THE BARN, Dylan watched as the kitchen cabinets were carried inside, knowing he should be helping, but he'd been avoiding being in Glory's vicinity as much as possible. Not that it was easy. She was there every day except Sunday, from early morning to late evening. It hadn't taken long to learn that she brought her lunch and ate while she worked. People had called him a workaholic, but they obviously hadn't seen her doing her job. At least he took time off for his dinner.

He was wondering what it was that drove her when his brother pulled in with the trailer behind his pickup and parked at the gate to the pasture. Dylan waited until Luke reached the barn to speak. "Any trouble?"

Luke shrugged. "A little with that one heifer, but she finally realized she was going to have to leave her baby behind, if she didn't get in the trailer. It didn't take long after that."

"Yeah, I bet it didn't."

Turning in the direction of the house, Luke asked, "So how's the redecorating going?"

"Is that what it's called?"

Luke looked over his shoulder. "I guess. That's what Hayley calls it, at least."

Dylan nodded.

"It's going okay?"

"I don't pay a lot of attention," Dylan answered. It was a lie. The truth was that he'd never intended to, but he did. A lot more than he liked. He didn't know much about decorating, but he knew at what point she was with the work in each of the rooms.

Except the upstairs bedrooms.

"She's working upstairs," he admitted.

Luke faced him, his eyes wide. "Yeah? What's she doing?"

"I'll be damned if I know. Stuff. All I know is that when Jim White was tearing out the old kitchen cabinets, she started asking questions about upstairs."

"You've been up there?" Luke asked.

"Just up the stairs," Dylan admitted. "She ordered me to stay out of the rooms."

Luke's eyebrows shot up. "Ordered? She *ordered* you?"

"Pretty much."

Luke ducked his head. "Glory never struck me as

someone who ordered other people around. It's like she just wished it and it was done."

When he looked up, Dylan could see that his brother was trying not to laugh. "Yeah, well, people change," he grumbled.

Laugh was exactly what Luke did, loud and long. "That's pretty obvious, at least where Glory's concerned."

"Right." Dylan didn't want to talk about it, and he couldn't look his brother in the eye when he said, "Let's get these cattle unloaded, instead of gossiping like a couple of old women."

He noticed a look on Luke's face that he couldn't quite understand, but he ignored it as they went to work. After they were done unloading the cattle, the two of them went into town for lunch. Instead of going home when they finished, Dylan stopped by his brother's house to spend some time with his nephew. He was amazed at how much Brayden had changed since Hayley had come into their lives. They were happy. Whenever he saw them all together, he'd have one of those "maybe someday" moments. Not that he thought he'd ever be a family man. He'd spent almost half his life working with his brother to make their ranch a success. And they had. He'd given up everything but ranching when his parents died, believing that was what they would have wanted. He owed them that much. There'd never been time for relaxing or even taking a woman out for dinner, but he hadn't thought about it. Until now.

Back at his ranch again, he managed to keep busy in and around the barn until it was getting too dark to see. He knew Glory was still working, but he'd run out of things to do to keep him away from the house. There was nothing left but to go inside and clean up. If he was lucky, Glory would be too busy upstairs to know that he'd come in, and she'd be gone by the time he'd showered and changed.

The kitchen was beginning to look as if it might survive the war Glory had waged on it. While it didn't look like the picture he'd seen, it had the same feel. Not that he needed that kind of kitchen. But now that Glory was making changes, he was beginning to think his sister had done the right thing when she'd hired Glory.

As he searched through the boxes in the dining room for a glass, he heard Glory's footsteps on the stairs. So much for that drink he'd planned to have.

"Oh, you're in," she said, stepping through the doorway and into the dining room. "Are you busy? Can you spare me a minute?"

"Sure," he answered, in spite of the wariness he felt.

Her smile was tentative and shy, and not at all like her. Then it was as if she shook it off and became the self-assured woman who'd walked into his kitchen three weeks before. "I'd like to show you something," she said, pointing toward the stairs behind her.

"Up there?"

She nodded. "It won't take long."

He shrugged. "Lead the way."

Following her up the stairs was an exercise in strength. It took everything he had not to watch her move from step to step. She always wore well-fitting jeans, but the view from just a few steps below nearly made him break out in a sweat. He was more than relieved when they reached the top and the view was more normal. Not that normal had been easy for him recently.

But being upstairs brought its own reaction. Until earlier that day, he hadn't been on the second floor for years. He took a deep breath and focused his attention on Glory while he spoke in what he hoped was a normal voice. "What is it you wanted to show me?"

Her wavering smile reappeared. "I've finished the first bedroom, and I'd like to get your opinion on it."

He couldn't imagine why she'd need to know what he thought. After all, he hadn't known the difference between Oyster and Creamy Ivory or even cared to. "I'll do what I can."

She opened the door to the room at the top of the stairs and walked in. He followed her, not knowing what to expect, but once he was inside, he could barely speak, except to say, "Wow."

The expression on her face as she looked at him was priceless. It was clear that his approval was important. He wasn't going to lie. There was no need to. "Wow," he repeated.

She moved farther into the room. "That's the same thing Brent said this morning."

For a moment he wasn't sure whom she was talking about. "Who?"

"Brent," she repeated. "One of the boys who's helping."

His relief surprised him. "Oh, yeah. Brent." It hadn't escaped him that whenever he saw the boys, they were falling all over themselves to help her. "You know, Glory," he said, feeling he should warn her about teenage boys, "a little encouragement might end up going further than you meant it to with those boys."

She cocked an eyebrow and put a hand on her hip. "Really?"

He decided maybe this wasn't the time to discuss the raging hormones of young boys, so he cleared his throat and searched for something to say. "So Brent said the same thing? 'Wow'?"

She ducked her head for a second before nodding. "I'm not sure what that means, though. It's one of those words that can have more than one meaning."

It was his turn to nod as he looked around the room, trying to take in everything. Nothing looked the same. In fact, he wasn't sure he was still in his house.

All but one wall was painted white, and that one was covered in a black-and-gray-and-white pattern he didn't have a name for. The two bedside tables and a chair near the windows—where curtains of the same pattern hung—were shiny black, as was the spread on the bed. It all looked…masculine, yet sophisticated, something he wasn't. But as the initial surprise wore off, he decided he liked it. A lot.

"What do you think?" she asked.

"I'm—" He groped for the right word. "I'm impressed."

Her eyes lit up. "You are?"

"Yeah," he answered, taking another long look around at everything. "Yeah, I am. Really impressed."

"It's all yours."

"I sure hope so."

She took a few steps toward him. "Try out the bed."

The word *bed* coming out of her mouth nearly knocked him over, and he took a step back. "That's okay. It looks good. It really does."

"You need to try it out," she said, taking his arm and pulling him toward the bed.

It was all he could do to keep from groaning out loud.

"It's brand-new," she said as they drew closer, "and I want to make sure it's comfortable for you."

"I can tell by looking that it is," he assured her as he tried to slow down their progress. It was the best he could do, under the circumstances, but it didn't work.

She let go of his arm and sat on the bed, bouncing. "You really need to try it. If it isn't right, I'll get it exchanged for something else."

He shook his head as he watched her bounce again, a teasing grin on her face. His mistake was closing his eyes, just for a moment, because when he did, she grabbed his hand and pulled him off balance, causing him to fall on the bed next to her. "Glory," he warned as things he shouldn't be thinking shot through his mind.

"How does it feel?"

"It feels fine," he said, through gritted teeth. He felt the bed beneath him move, and knew she'd caused it. "Just fine. Now—"

"You're just saying that. Try it out right. Please?"

Nobody had ever been able to say no to Glory Caldwell. He knew it, all the guys knew it and even Glory herself was probably aware of it. But rolling over on his back could be the end of a lot of things. Instead, he pushed himself into a sitting position as he rolled over. There was no reason to let her know exactly what being near her was doing to him.

"It's great, Glory—it really is."

She groaned and fell backward on the bed, beside him. "Really, Dylan, you aren't helping."

"*I'm* not helping?" He not only barely realized he'd spoken, but he was leaning over her, gazing into the face that he'd dreamed about as a teenager, more than once. Without thinking, he leaned closer, ready to taste the lips turned up in a tempting, almost seductive smile.

The realization of what was happening shot through him like a bolt of lightning, and he jerked away. Beside him, she moved.

"Dylan?"

When she touched his arm, he forced himself to get

to his feet, but he didn't look at her. "It's great, Glory—it really is. I'm sure I'll sleep like I've never slept before."

He heard a soft gasp and felt movement on the bed behind him, and then she hurried past him to the door. "I'm sorry, Dylan," she said, her voice cracking. "I shouldn't have— I didn't mean to— It won't happen again."

He couldn't move or even call her back. Of course it wouldn't happen again. He couldn't let it. What would she say if she knew what he'd done fifteen years ago?

Chapter Four

Glory climbed the stairs to the upper floor of the shop, looking for something to keep her busy. Although it was midafternoon, the light was dim, thanks to a late-spring storm, complete with lightning and thunder loud enough to wake her in the middle of the night. That was all it had taken to convince her that she should take a day off.

She desperately needed some time away. If she'd gone to work, it would have been next to impossible for her to steer clear of Dylan, thanks to the rain. She suspected he would do pretty much anything to avoid her. She deserved it. After making a fool of herself while showing him his bedroom, what did she think would happen? But she hadn't been thinking. And that was the problem.

Determined to put it out of her mind, she did a slow turn in the middle of the low-ceilinged room. She'd been in the midst of sorting things when Erin had called her and given her the go-ahead to meet with Dylan and start work. Since then, she'd been out at the Walker house almost every day, so nothing much had been done at the shop.

The sound of rain on the roof was comforting, but she shuddered at the damp chill in the unfinished room. With luck, she remembered seeing an old dusty cardigan sweater in one of the boxes. Digging it out, she wrapped herself in it, and then skirted around several boxes and chairs to plug in an antique floor lamp in the far corner. It took a moment to find the switch, but to her delight, the bulb burned brightly when she turned it on, casting shadows around the room.

She didn't feel like working, so when she found a box full of old picture frames of all sizes, she settled cross-legged on the floor and pulled the box closer. Most were empty of pictures, but some had pressed flowers and clippings of pretty quotes. Thinking they might come in handy someday, she set the box near the stairs.

When she heard footsteps, she called to her grandmother. "I thought you were going to stay home and out of the rain."

"I tried," Louise said when she reached the top step, "but I kept thinking of you here all alone and wondering if there might be something I could help you with."

Glory moved the box out of the way and got to her feet. "I'm not really doing anything, just—"

"Avoiding Dylan Walker?"

Whipping her head around, she stared at her grandmother. "Why would I do that?"

Louise replied with a shrug. "I don't know. Maybe you can tell *me*."

Glory gave a dismissive wave as she walked past her grandmother to the stairs. "You're imagining things. With this wet weather, trying to paint or hang wallpaper would be a waste of time. I might as well be here or spending time with you."

"If you say so," Louise said, following her down the stairs. Once they were in the main shop, she walked to the wide window that looked out onto Main Street.

"I don't know why, but ice cream sounds good, don't you think?"

"Heavenly," Glory answered, looking out at the gray skies and the cars splashing water in the street as they drove by. "If only there was somewhere we could get some."

"You've been gone from Desperation too long, my girl."

Glory looked at her. "What do you mean?"

"It's time to catch you up on all the new things in town."

"Such as?"

"The Sweet and Yummy Ice Cream Parlor."

"Really?" Glory chuckled at the name. "How cute! Ice cream it is, then. We'll take my car." Slipping off the dusty sweater, she grabbed her jacket from a chair.

Louise stopped on her way to the door. "Car? My dear girl, do I look like I can't walk a few blocks?"

Glory picked up her bag. "Of course not, Gram, but—"

"Just because I'm barely past my sixties, it doesn't mean I'm infirm."

"Gram, it's raining."

"So it is." Louise pulled two umbrellas from a box in the corner and handed one to Glory, with a look that asked if there would be any other excuses.

Glory took the umbrella in one hand and looped her other arm with her grandmother's. "We'd better lock up."

"Nobody's going to bother this old shop."

But Glory didn't want to risk it. Her future was inside the old building, and she didn't intend to give anyone the chance to harm her dream.

Outside, with the door secured, Louise pointed to the right, and they turned to walk in that direction.

Glory hadn't had much time to reacquaint herself with the town where she'd spent the first nineteen years of her life. Now that she had a free day to catch up, she was surprised to see the changes Desperation had undergone. If she hadn't gotten married, if she hadn't moved away with her new husband to chase his big-city dreams, she might never have left. Kyle had achieved his dream, and then wanted more. She'd simply been the good little wife he'd expected. That mistake wouldn't be repeated.

"I see they gave the fire station a new coat of paint," she commented as they walked along the sidewalk.

"Some time ago, if I recollect," Louise answered.

"So where's this ice-cream place?"

Louise turned to look at her, a twinkle in her bright blue eyes. "You'll see."

"A surprise?"

"I think *you'll* be surprised."

As they walked on, Glory noticed the familiar places that had been a part of her life. They passed the post office and the doctor's office. There were new businesses, too, while some had moved. She spied an older building that had been similar to a general store, but was now a freshly painted day care center. The laughter of the children coming from inside prompted a smile.

"Oh, my!" she cried when she saw an elderly man hurrying down the street. "Is that Vern?"

"It is," Louise answered.

"And there's Esther," Glory said with a sigh. "Following him." She turned to her grandmother. "Hasn't she ever caught him?"

"Not that anyone knows," Louise answered.

Glory shook her head. "It's hard to believe. I remember seeing Esther chasing him around town when I was a little girl." She silently hoped that she'd be there to see it when Esther finally caught him, but with the two of them in their eighties, she wasn't sure that would be likely.

They passed by the new library, which had been located in the city building and was now in a big, new building of its own, with brightly colored posters of available books and notices of upcoming activities both there and around town.

"Here we are."

Busy reading the flyers and posters in the library windows, Glory turned to see her grandmother pointing across the street to what had long ago been the pride of the town—the Opera House. Even when she was a small child the building had shown the wear and tear of the years, and a sadness had seemed to wrap around it. But it only took a moment to realize that the large building had received some much-needed work. Windows that had once been boarded up were now sparkling in the afternoon sunshine.

"Surprised?" Louise asked as they crossed the street.

"Completely. When did this happen?"

Louise led her past the first recessed doorway to another as she explained the long process of the renovation that had taken place. "The businesses here in the front started opening about three years ago, and then Kate Clayborne and Dusty McPherson had their wedding reception in the theater itself, just before Christmas that same year, although it wasn't completely finished yet."

"Dusty married Kate?" Glory was more surprised about that than the grand new look of the Opera House. Dusty had been in her class, although he hadn't always lived in Desperation. And Kate...well, Kate had been an odd girl, who'd moved from across the state with her sister to live with their aunt, after they'd lost their parents in a tornado. "What I remember most about Kate was that she chopped off all her glorious red hair."

Louise passed through the doorway, chuckled and pointed to a sign a little farther down the long hallway. "That's her bakery and catering business. She keeps busy. She and Dusty have twin boys."

Glory stopped to stare at the sign, stunned at how much she had missed. "Amazing. What about her sister?"

"Trish married Desperation's sheriff. But then I don't think you've met Morgan Rule yet."

"No, I haven't," Glory answered, trying to catch her memories up with the present. "And this is the ice-cream parlor?"

As Louise walked through the open door, Glory's cell phone alerted her to a call. "I'll be right in," she told her grandmother. When she pulled the phone from her purse and saw it was Dylan's number, her hand trembled.

"The new appliances have arrived, but the cabinets aren't finished yet," he said, after she answered. "I don't know what you want these men who delivered them to do. Can you come out to the ranch?"

Seeing him wasn't what she'd planned, but neither could she shirk her duties. "I'll be there in a few minutes. Ask them to please wait, would you?"

He assured her he would, and with a sigh of resignation, she stepped into the Sweet and Yummy Ice Cream Parlor to tell her grandmother she wouldn't be able to enjoy the treat with her, after all. Business came first, no matter how much she wanted to avoid it.

WHILE THE SUN battled with the last of the clouds left from the thunderstorm, Dylan stood in the soggy yard, waiting for Glory to arrive. Early that morning, she'd sent him a message, saying that because of the rain she wouldn't be at the ranch today. That had been fine with him. He needed the time to get his head straight.

There'd been only one problem. He realized that he missed seeing her working at the house, even though he usually tried to steer clear of her. Getting close to someone wasn't a good idea. He had a ranch to run, and a woman—especially one like Glory—took a lot of time and attention he couldn't afford.

"Is that her?" one of the deliverymen asked.

Looking toward the road that ran by the house, Dylan felt a funny little skip in his chest, but he ignored it. But it wasn't Glory's car that drove past and continued on around the curve. "It may take her a few minutes," he said. "She may have—"

He didn't need to finish as her bright blue car turned into the lane, splashing muddy water that had collected in the dips of the rock-lined lane. His first thought was that she needed to slow down. His second was that he needed to not care.

The two deliverymen and the carpenter, who'd been waiting on the front porch, scrambled to their feet as the car came to a stop.

"Don't need no sun with her around," one of the men said when Glory climbed out of the car.

Dylan pretended he didn't hear the comment, but if he'd been foolish enough to reply, he would have agreed. Knowing he wasn't the only one affected by her didn't necessarily help.

Sidestepping puddles of water, she approached the house. Her smile, both blinding and apologetic, included all four men. Dylan didn't return it, but the others did.

"Mr. Walker tells me we have a problem," she announced, coming to a stop in front of him.

Dylan wasn't sure whether or not to be pleased she hadn't called him by his given name. It was as if this was her way of telling him they were all business, the two of them. No hanky-panky. No, sir.

"We're at least a week away from being able to put in those appliances," the carpenter doing the cabinets said, with a nod at the truck sitting a few yards away. "Probably longer. The thing is I don't think these boys here are too excited about taking them back until we're ready for them."

Glory glanced at Dylan. "And it would cost Mr. Walker extra to do that, I'm sure. No, we need to find a place where they can be kept. If possible."

Dylan was sure she was hoping he'd come to her rescue, but he wasn't anybody's white knight.

"We can't sit here much longer," one of the deliverymen said with a glance at the other. "There's other customers we need to get to today."

The carpenter shook his head. "There's no room in the kitchen. I can't work around them, and something might happen if I tried. I know you don't want a bunch of dented and scratched appliances, Mr. Walker."

Tempted to tell the man that it didn't make any difference to him what his appliances looked like, Dylan kept quiet. He'd never been the type to be rude or to hurt someone's feelings, especially someone like Glory, who didn't deserve it.

"Is that a machine shed over there?" the other deliveryman asked. When Dylan nodded, he continued. "Would it be possible to keep them in there, until it's time to install them? If there's room for them, that is."

Before Dylan could answer, Glory spoke. "I suppose

that would mean an additional charge for returning to hook them up?"

The man nodded.

"Drive on around to the machine shed," Dylan said.

Glory took a step toward him. "But——"

"I'll meet you both back there and give you a hand with them," he continued. When they started for the truck, he turned to the carpenter. "Don't worry about rushing the work to get those appliances in. We'll get them in when the time comes."

The man nodded and walked toward the house, leaving Dylan to deal with Glory. "Just how did this mix-up happen?"

She squared her shoulders and looked him in the eye. "It was my fault. I didn't calculate enough time for the new cabinets. I'll pay the charge for the return trip to connect——"

"No, you won't."

"But——"

"Luke and I can get them in and hook them up."

She shook her head. "It's not your responsibility. It was my mistake and I intend to take——"

"Full responsibility," he finished for her. "Yeah, I know. I'll keep that in mind when we're hooking up all that newfangled stuff."

"That's not right. It was——"

"Glory," he said, his patience wearing thin, "it's my house, and I haven't done anything to help out with any of this."

"It's my job, what I'm paid to do. I was the one who messed up."

He noticed the bright pink splotches coloring her cheeks, and he realized he'd somehow embarrassed her, although he didn't know exactly what he'd said or done. He wasn't sure what to do about it, either.

He grabbed the first excuse he could think of to get away, before he made things worse. "I have to go help unload," he said, "but don't leave. We'll get this settled." When she looked away and didn't answer, he asked, "Okay?"

After hesitating, she nodded, but still didn't look directly at him. "I'll be inside."

She'd turned away before he had a chance to say more. As he headed for the machine shed to help unload the appliances, it hit him that Glory had a stubborn streak almost as long and wide as his. It would do her well in the business world. She wouldn't be the type of person who'd let anyone push her around. But it sure wasn't the Glory he remembered. Everyone had called her sweet and pleasant. But now? He wasn't so sure.

By the time he reached the machine shed, the only thing left was the monstrous box that contained the refrigerator. It was a good thing he was there to help with it. Even with all three of them and the lift on the back of the truck, the job wasn't easy. When they finished, the men reminded him to call when they were ready to move the things to the house, and he assured them he would. It was a lie, but he couldn't think of a reason to tell them the truth. In a week, they'd forget all about the Walker appliances.

In the kitchen, the carpenter pointed toward the living room before Dylan could ask about Glory. Determined to settle the question of who would install the appliances, he stepped into the living room, and his heart jumped to his throat.

Glory, perched at the top of a wobbly stepladder, was reaching higher for what he guessed was a loose strip of wallpaper. His first instinct was to call out to her, but he immediately stopped himself, thinking that doing so might cause her to lose her balance.

Instead, he quietly approached the ladder. When he was within reach of it, he spoke, keeping his voice low and as matter-of-fact as he could, ready to catch her, if needed. "We need to find you something better to climb on."

She turned slightly and looked down at him as he grasped the ladder to steady it. "I've always been a climber," she said.

His breath caught at the sight of her as beams of sunlight from a nearby window turned her hair to pure gold. At that moment, his only thought was to reach up and pull her down to him and finish that kiss he'd nearly started the day before. Lucky for him, common sense took over. "Maybe you have, but I don't need you suing me when something happens. Come on down."

"Who's suing who?"

Dylan turned toward the sound of the voice and saw that Luke, who had asked the question, was standing with Hayley in the kitchen doorway.

"He's right, you know," Hayley said. "These ten-foot ceilings make reaching them more difficult, even with a ladder."

"A small scaffold would do the trick," Luke suggested.

Dylan, grateful for the interruption, agreed. "Come on down, Glory. We'll find something safer for you to use."

"The boys set up a scaffold for me upstairs," she said when she reached the floor.

"The boys?" Dylan asked.

She nodded. "Mark, Stu and Brent."

"Oh, they did, huh?"

She looked up at him, frowning. "They've been a huge help," she said, and then turned to his brother with a smile. "It's always good to see you, Luke. And I'm guessing this is your soon-to-be bride?"

Luke put an arm around Hayley. "This is Hayley."

Hayley stepped forward and offered her hand as Glory walked toward her. "I've heard a lot about you, Glory. I guess it's been a long time since you've been back."

Glory took her hand and nodded. "It has. The last time I was here was ten years ago to visit my mom. She lives in Texas now." She released Hayley's hand and looked in Dylan's direction, but not at him. "If it's all right, I'd like to wash my hands and get a cold drink of water."

"Sure."

Dylan watched as she walked past his brother and future sister-in-law, but instead of hearing the sound of water at the sink, he heard the faint closing of the screen door on the porch.

"Is she upset about something?" Luke asked.

Dylan wondered what excuse he could give. "We had a little disagreement about the appliances, earlier."

"I'd get that cleared up right away."

He looked at his brother. "Yeah, I'll do that." But there was something about the way Luke was looking at him. Did his brother think there was something going on between him and Glory? If so, he was wrong. Dylan had no intention of letting that happen.

GRATEFUL TO BE too busy to worry about anything beyond the work, Glory moved from the finished bedroom to the former bedroom. When she was done, Dylan would have an office that would not only be utilitarian, but a room where she hoped he would be comfortable. She envisioned a place where he could not only find the papers for the ranch's latest cattle acquisition or sale, but keep the massive collection of books she'd discovered in what had probably been a pantry. She'd never tell anyone, but a man who read was one of her biggest turn-ons. As if she needed that.

"You're sure you want a wall from this doorway all the way to that outside wall, Miz Andrews?"

Glory nodded at the handyman. "I'll need a door—" she ran a measured glance down what would be a hall- way "—about here. I'll give you the measurements later."

The man scratched his chin and slowly moved his head from side to side. "I guess I don't get it, what with shortening the hall down there by the bathroom."

With patience she wasn't feeling at the moment, she explained that the space would be a closet, accessible from the office. His answer was a shrug, and she worried she'd need to keep a close eye on him. Not only was there a hall being added, but both bathrooms, upstairs and downstairs, were getting a face-lift, making things a bit inconvenient for a while. The only room that wasn't having much done was the dining room. She'd fallen in love with the dining table and chairs and refused to remove them from the house. If Dylan didn't like it, he could do whatever he wanted after she'd finished the job.

She was in the dining room, which she secretly called her command post, working with the floor plans she'd had drawn up for the new office, when she heard the porch door open and close. She didn't need to look to know it was Dylan. The sound of his footsteps had become far too familiar. She'd slipped the pictures she was using for her decorating scheme beneath a fat notebook when the footsteps stopped. Looking up, she discovered him standing in the doorway.

"Don't you ever take a break?" he asked.

"Of course I do. Not on a regular schedule, but when I need one I take it."

"What about lunch?"

She pointed toward her large canvas bag in the corner. "I bring my lunch. Why?"

He shrugged, his gaze going around the room, but skipping right past her. "Ned said the kitchen would be ready for the appliances in a few days."

Ned? She was surprised he knew the carpenter's name. "That's good news, considering we thought it would be longer."

"He's a good worker. Seems to know what he's doing."

She wasn't sure how to answer, so she nodded and pretended to study the plans in front of her. Had he thought she would be clueless? He should know that in a small town, finding good workers was the easy part. Fred Mercer at the hardware store was a wealth of knowledge, but although she trusted him, she also double-checked his suggestions with Gram and others. It always paid to get both a man's view and a woman's. Each saw things a little differently.

Taking a peek from beneath her lashes, she saw that Dylan was watching her, and her body reacted with a flash of heat. If she couldn't get herself under control, she didn't know how she was going to finish the job.

She raised her head to look directly at him and hoped he didn't notice how rattled she was by his continued presence. "Was there something else?"

"What? No, nothing. Nothing except I was wondering if you had any idea when this would all be done."

So he was in a hurry to get rid of her. Well, she'd take all the time she needed and didn't care what he thought. "I'll know better in a week or so."

He nodded. "Yeah. Okay. I just..." Instead of finishing whatever it was he was going to say, he turned and left the room.

When she was certain he was gone, she put her hands on the table and braced herself. Her knees were shaking so badly she could hardly stand. He wasn't making this easy on her. She was doing the best she could. In fact, she felt she was doing an excellent job. If she could just finish it up, they'd both be happier.

By late afternoon, she'd given the promised measurements to the handyman for the wall and started packing the leftovers from what had been Dylan's bedroom. There were already several boxes along the wall where the bed had been, apparently packed by Dylan, and she tested the nearest one to make sure it wasn't too heavy for her to lift. Finding them light enough, she carried it to the pantry, and then returned for another.

When she started to pick up the second one, she heard the sound of glass rattling in it. Wondering what it could be and hoping nothing had broken, she knelt on the floor and picked up the folded newspaper sitting on top of the box. What she saw sent a wave of disappointment through her.

Liquor. Several bottles of it. Too many, in fact. Her father had been and probably still was a functioning alcoholic.

Reaching into the box, she pulled out one of the bottles and noticed the half-full tumbler sitting behind the box. Picking it up with her other hand, she sighed.

"What are you doing?"

She nearly dropped both the glass and the bottle as she jerked her head up. "I was—I was moving the boxes into the pantry."

Dylan walked into the room and leaned down, taking the bottle and glass from her hands. "I'll take care of it."

She didn't want to look at him. It was none of her business. She was there to do a job and had no right to judge him on what he did with his life.

She shook her head. "I've got it. Just put the bottle in the box with the others."

"It has nothing to do with you."

He was right—it didn't—but that didn't seem to help quell her disappointment in him. She couldn't risk looking at him. He would immediately know how she felt.

Clearing her throat, she got to her feet. "If you'll hand me the box, I'll put it in the pantry with the other things."

Without meaning to, she looked up and saw him watching her, his green eyes unreadable.

"All right."

For a second, she wasn't sure she'd heard him, and then she realized he'd agreed. He picked up the box and handed it to her. With nothing more she could say, she thanked him and vowed to put the incident behind her. He was right. It had nothing to do with her.

Chapter Five

Dylan stood at the pasture fence and looked out over the best of the herd. He should have been feeling good. He and his brother had come a long way over the past fifteen years. They'd taken a small family ranch that had barely made enough to keep the five of them fed and clothed, with little left over for extras, and they'd turned it into a successful cattle operation that had garnered the attention of some of the best cattlemen in three states. But that wasn't what was on his mind.

He couldn't stop thinking about the look on Glory's face the day before, the half-empty glass of bourbon in her hand. He'd told himself it didn't matter and that he could do whatever he wanted. But her disappointment had gotten to him, no matter how much he'd tried to tell himself it hadn't.

He heard his brother call his name, and he turned his head, hoping to erase the image in his mind. "What's the plan?"

Luke joined him at the fence, propping his booted foot on the rail next to Dylan's. "It's Saturday."

"Right. So?"

"Fresh barbecue at Lou's Place."

Dylan nodded. "You're right. I hadn't thought of that.

It's been a while since I've stopped in for one of Kate's barbecued beef sandwiches."

"Same here."

Dylan pushed away from the fence and stepped back. "Then I'd better get cleaned up."

Luke laughed. "I thought you might say that. I'll meet you there."

After Luke turned to leave, Dylan started for the house. He'd only taken a few steps when he remembered that Glory was inside with one of the contractors she'd hired to fix up the bathrooms. She'd told him before he headed out earlier that morning that the water would be off, so taking a shower before going to Lou's was out of the question.

"Hey, Luke," he called. "Mind if I take a shower at your place?"

Luke waved and answered. "Fine with me. Hayley took Brayden to see her folks, and they won't be back for a couple of days."

"I'll see you in a few minutes, then," Dylan answered.

Inside, he grabbed a fresh set of clothes from his bedroom, and discovered Glory in the next room, touching up the freshly painted walls. His first instinct was to keep going and hope she didn't notice. Instead, he stopped in the doorway.

She must have sensed he was there, because she turned around. "Oh, I didn't hear you."

Cussing himself because he'd been fool enough to stop, he searched for something to say. He considered asking if he could bring her something back from Lou's, but vetoed the idea. She might think he was trying to win her approval or something. He wasn't. He couldn't care less about that. "I'll be at Lou's Place with Luke, after I clean up at his house, if anyone needs to know."

He noticed again that her usual smile was more a frown than anything, and she didn't look at him when she spoke. "I was afraid something would come up while the water is turned off."

"No big deal. It isn't like Luke's place is out of the way."

She nodded, and then turned back to the wall.

He didn't have any doubt that her obvious disapproval was because of what had happened the day before. "This is my house, you know," he said, the words spilling from his mouth.

She glanced over her shoulder at him and answered, "Yes, it is," and then went back to her painting.

Wishing he hadn't bothered to stop or even look in the doorway as he passed, he walked out of the room and down the stairs. Next time, he'd know better.

Within a few minutes, he pulled his pickup into the drive at Luke's home, a mile down the road from his, and parked, thinking about lunch. It was much safer to do that than think of Glory, with that smudge of paint on her nose.

He'd been angry with her the day before, when she'd found the bottles. Now he felt guilty about it. Was he crazy?

Thirty minutes later, showered and dressed in clean clothes, and riding in Luke's pickup, they pulled into the parking lot at Lou's Place, Desperation's local tavern. "You're looking kind of down in the mouth," Luke said as he pulled into an empty spot. "Something bothering you?"

Dylan swore under his breath. His brother knew him too well. He wasn't about to tell him or anyone else what had happened. "Nope," he answered. "I was just thinking how hungry I am and hoping there's plenty of food left."

"You and me both." Shutting off the engine, Luke reached for the door handle and grinned. "Let's go get us some barbecue."

Dylan nodded and opened the door on his side, determined to keep his mind on anything but Glory. He'd spent a sleepless night dealing with the memory of the look on her face when he'd found her with the bottles. He wasn't an alcoholic, no matter what she might think. Except for an occasional beer with friends, the only time he drank was once a year, when his guilt about his parents' accident was more than he could handle. If he'd been where he was supposed to be that day, fifteen years ago, his mother would be enjoying the grandson she'd never had a chance to know and his father would be reaping the benefits of a successful ranch. And he and his sister and brother would still have their parents.

Glory had made him realize that the drinking had to stop. He would never be able to forget, or stop missing his mom and dad, but he could do that much to make things right. Even if Glory might never know, he'd made a silent promise that morning that his annual binge-drinking days were over.

"You're sure everything's all right?" Luke asked.

As they walked toward the tavern, Dylan shook off the dark thoughts. "Right as rain."

"How's the decorating stuff going?" Luke asked when they reached the door.

"Okay."

Luke looked over his shoulder as he opened the door and walked inside. "Just okay?"

Dylan stepped through behind his brother. "It's hard to tell. The house is pretty much a mess."

"Hayley's curious to see how it's going."

Dylan shrugged. "Glory might like the company. She might put her to work, though."

Luke laughed as they greeted a handful of friends and neighbors on their way to a table in a corner. "I doubt she'd mind." Taking a seat, he looked around. "Busy place today."

Dylan chose a spot at the table where he could see the comings and goings, and then signaled one of the waitresses. "I guess this is when we'll find out if they've run out of barbecue."

"I'm hoping luck is on our side." Luke turned to the waitress, who had just walked up to the table. "Hey, Lucy."

"Hi, boys. What can I get you?"

"Two draws." He glanced at Dylan, who nodded and then held up three fingers. "And six of Kate's sandwiches. If there are any left."

She smiled. "At least enough left for both of you. I'll be back with them in a few minutes."

"Thanks." When she walked away, he turned to Dylan. "Now there's a nice girl. Maybe you should give some thought to—"

"No, thanks."

"Got your eye on Glory, huh?"

Dylan snorted. "Yeah, like I'm that crazy." Considering what had happened the day before, even if he'd been interested, he'd blown his chance. Not that it mattered, he reminded himself. He didn't have any interest in getting tangled up with Glory or anyone else.

Luke leaned a little closer. "I think she likes you."

Dylan slowly turned his head to stare at his brother.

"Glory," Luke answered, as if Dylan hadn't understood.

"Glory likes everybody," Dylan replied, without looking him in the eye. "She always has. So don't go gettin' any ideas, because there's no reason. Got it?"

Luke leaned back in his chair and held up both hands in surrender. "Whatever you say."

Dylan spied Dusty coming in the door with another cowboy and waved a hand to indicate the empty seats at their table. "Plenty of room here," Dylan said.

"Save a seat for Morgan," Dusty said, claiming a chair. "He'll be here as soon as his shift is over. Tanner and Tucker, too."

"No wives?" Luke asked.

Dusty shook his head. "They're busy working on stuff for the box social."

"Hayley mentioned something about that," Luke said. "I haven't been to one for a long time."

Totally in the dark about what they were talking about, Dylan leaned forward. "Does somebody want to let me in on this box thing?"

Dusty turned to him. "You're kidding, right?"

Shaking his head, Dylan looked around the table at the others. "No. Should I know about this?"

Sheriff Morgan Rule walked up to the table, pulled out a chair and joined them. "Every man in the vicinity of Desperation knows the annual box social is the best place to get a fine meal. The ladies always manage to outdo themselves each year."

Dusty pointed at the cowboy next to him. "Even Jeff here is seriously considering coming back next weekend for it."

Looking at Dusty's friend, Dylan realized the man wasn't a stranger. He and Luke had known Jeff Morton for several years, having met him at a rodeo where their sister was competing. He'd been an up-and-coming bull rider before an injury had slowed him down, although he still did some competing. But from what Dylan had heard, Jeff's main interest was a cattle ranch in Colorado.

Lucy appeared with Luke's and Dylan's orders, then took the orders of the other men at the table. "These will probably be the last barbecue sandwich orders I'll be able to fill. There's been a big crowd today, and that's what everyone is ordering."

When she walked away, Dylan turned to Jeff. "You still riding?"

Jeff leaned back in his chair. "Some. In fact, I ran into your sister a couple of months ago."

"Yeah?" Luke asked.

Jeff nodded. "Yeah. She was showing me a saddle made here in Desperation some years ago. She'd just bought it from a relative of the saddle maker."

Dylan sat up straighter and leaned forward. "Did you say Erin bought the saddle?" He glanced at Luke, whose eyebrows lifted slightly. "Did she mention any names?"

Shaking his head, Jeff took a sip of his beer before answering. "None that I recall."

Dylan looked at Luke again. It was obvious to Dylan that his brother noticed the same coincidence he did. Glory's grandfather had to have made the saddle. "Would you know the name if you heard it?"

"Maybe," Jeff answered with a shrug.

Dylan nodded when Luke glanced at him. "Could it have been Gardner?" Luke asked.

Jeff's eyes narrowed. "You know, I can't say for certain that it was."

Dylan glanced at Luke, who had turned to talk to Morgan, giving no indication that he was listening.

With his radar up over the sale to his sister of a saddle that may or may not have been Glory's, Dylan knew the only way to find out was to call Erin and try to get some information from her. Even if it wasn't a saddle that had belonged to Glory, it was fairly obvious that it had been made by Abe Gardner, who'd made some of the best saddles in a five-state area, and was probably worth a good-sized chunk of money.

When Dylan pushed away from the table, Luke turned to look at him, pointing at Dylan's lunch. "Where are you going? You haven't finished."

Dylan pulled out his cell phone. "I'll finish it in a few minutes. I need to make a call."

"Dylan," Luke called. But Dylan walked away and didn't answer, focused on what he was going to say to his sister when she answered the phone.

The number rang several times, and he was just about to give up when Erin answered. "Hey, Dylan, what's up?"

"Maybe you can tell me. Did you buy a saddle Abe Gardner made?"

"How'd you hear about it?" she asked, without answering his question.

"Jeff Morton. He just said he'd run into you and that you'd mentioned buying a saddle."

Her grunt held contempt. "Where'd you run into Jeff?"

He heard voices in the background and his sister saying something, so he waited to answer. "He's here at Lou's with Dusty," he said when it was quiet again.

"What is it you wanted to know?" she asked.

He could tell she was distracted. "Did you buy a saddle that Abe Gardner made?"

Once again, there was the sound of people in the background. "Listen, Dylan, I can't talk now," she said.

He didn't like to be put off. "But—"

"Yeah, I bought one of Abe's saddles. We'll talk about it some other time."

He could tell by the silence that she'd hung up, so he made sure the call was disconnected, pocketed the phone and strode to the table.

"Who were you talking to?" Luke asked when Dylan took his seat at the table.

"Erin. I was trying to find out who she bought the saddle from."

"Did you?"

Dylan shook his head and reached for his beer. "No, she had to go."

"So you don't know who the saddle belonged to, just that Abe made it?" When Dylan nodded, Luke asked, "Are you thinking it was Glory's?"

"Could be," Dylan said. "But I'll find out."

He had more questions for his sister and would get to the bottom of it, just as soon as he got home. But for now, Dusty was pulling his chair around to sit next to him.

Giving Dylan a friendly slap on the back, Dusty said, "Now, about that box social next Saturday…"

LEAVING THE WALKER ranch earlier than usual before Dylan returned, Glory scolded herself for being relieved that he'd been gone most of the day. She couldn't help it. Spending any time with him so soon after she'd found what she suspected was a secret stash was impossible. She'd tried to hide her disappointment, but she knew she hadn't succeeded. She also knew it was none of her business, and if it had been anyone else, she would have forgotten about it. That meant only one thing. She cared about him more than she wanted to admit, and that wasn't good.

Needing to get her mind off her troubles, she remembered the bakery her grandmother had pointed out during their trip to the ice-cream parlor and decided to see if it was open. A pie would make a nice dessert for later, and her grandmother would enjoy it. Besides, she might get a glimpse of Kate Clayborne.

Inside the historic building, the Open sign was visible in the frosted glass door of the bakery. Peering through a window, she could see long, curly auburn hair and knew instantly that it belonged to Kate.

As she turned the doorknob and stepped inside, a jingling chorus sounded overhead as the aroma of pies, cakes and cookies filled her head. Looking up, she smiled at the sight of a group of sleigh bells hanging from the top of the door. If what she remembered about Kate still held true, she should have expected something out of the ordinary.

"Very pretty," she said.

The redhead behind the counter turned around, and her face broke out in a wide smile. "Glory Caldwell Andrews. I can't believe it's you."

"I could say the same for you, Kate Clayborne McPherson."

Kate shook her head and laughed. "Amazing. I'm surprised you remember me."

"You were unforgettable." Glory hoped Kate wouldn't take her words the wrong way, but there was something in the way she smiled that assured her that wouldn't happen.

"I'm truly honored," Kate replied.

It was Glory's turn to laugh. "And just why is that?"

"Well, after all, besides being the most popular girl in school, you were a senior, and I was a lowly freshman."

"True," Glory said, struggling to keep a straight face. "I'm just happy to see that your hair grew out."

"Aha!" Kate cried. "I knew you'd remember that. But then I don't think there's anyone in town that doesn't." She propped her elbows on the counter and rested her chin in her hands. "It's really good to see you home again."

Home. Glory felt a quick stab of wistfulness for all the things she'd missed by marrying and moving so far away, but she quickly brushed it aside. "Word spreads fast."

"It does. I hear you're doing some work over at the Walker place. How's that going?"

Glory wasn't sure how to answer. At the moment, she was wondering if she'd been crazy to take the job. Then again, she knew she was doing a good job, in spite of Dylan's nonparticipation in the process. "It's coming along."

"That's what Dylan said when we saw him in the café last week."

"He mentioned it?"

"Briefly. He isn't much of a talker."

Smiling, Glory shrugged one shoulder. "No, he isn't, but he never was, as I remember. He's even more serious now than when we were all in school."

Kate nodded. "I guess it's kind of expected. After the accident and all."

"I guess." Glory knew Dylan's emotional condition was really none of her business—just as his drinking habits weren't, either. She didn't want Kate to think she was overcurious, so she changed the topic. "So you married Dusty," she said. "He was such a bad boy."

"Wasn't he?" Kate said, with a soft chuckle. "So the bad boy and the crazy girl hooked up."

"Stranger things have happened." Glory had no room to talk about things like that and wondered what Kate would think if she answered that it wasn't any stranger than the Prom Queen marrying the Prom King, who then cheated on her for the entire seven years they were married.

Instead of thinking about her miserable marriage, Glory thought about happier times. Sometimes they seemed like a lifetime ago, but at that moment, they seemed like yesterday. "Good times," she said.

"They were. Looking back, anyway. And speaking of good times, do you have your basket ready?"

"Basket?" Glory asked. "I thought Easter was earlier in the year."

Kate reached across the counter and tapped her on the arm. "For the annual box social, silly."

Although she and Kate had never been more than acquaintances, just girls who had attended the same small school, talking to her was like talking to an old friend. Life was strange. First Dylan, and now Kate. But the box social? She didn't have a reason to participate.

"No, no basket," she replied.

Kate pressed a hand to her heart and the back of her other hand to her forehead. "Please say you're kidding!" She leaned across the counter. "You have to have a basket! You're single, and it's almost a law that single women are required to participate." Her eyes widened for a moment, then she straightened and pressed her lips together as she looked away, obviously embarrassed.

"So everyone knows?" Glory asked, keeping her voice low as if that would stop the gossip.

Kate shrugged, but didn't look directly at her. "You know how it is in small towns."

"So what are they saying?"

"Only that you're back and Kyle isn't, and it appears to be permanent."

Glory nodded, knowing that an explanation would be needed at some point. But she wasn't going to offer it or think about it until she had to. "That's fair. But I really didn't come in to catch up on the latest gossip. I need to get a pie or something for dessert tonight."

Kate ducked behind the counter and reappeared with a delicious-looking lattice-crust cherry pie, but didn't set it on the counter. "Now, back to your basket for the box social…"

"No basket," Glory replied, standing firm.

Kate turned the pie around slowly, with a smile so conniving, there was no doubt what she was up to. "No basket, no pie."

Glory tried a new tactic, hoping this one would work. "I don't even know what I'd put in a basket."

"Then I'll help you."

Shaking her head, Glory sighed. "I'm beyond hope, Kate. It's been forever since I've made anything from scratch."

Kate leaned closer. "I'll provide the dessert. Nobody needs to know. And I'm sure we can come up with something you can make. It isn't like it has to be a gourmet meal. The food isn't the best part. It's who bids on the basket and wins."

Glory couldn't imagine anybody bidding on something she'd cooked. "I hope they're accustomed to food poisoning."

Laughing, Kate put the pie down and flashed a

wicked grin. "Honey, with my cooking skills and your decorating flair, you'll have the best basket there."

"Oh, all right," Glory said with a sigh, giving in. "What do we need to do?" But she worried that she was getting herself into something she'd soon regret. Not only that, but she wondered if Kate Clayborne McPherson was as crazy as she'd been fifteen years before.

DYLAN FELT HIS tension evaporate when he pulled up in front of the ranch. Dusk was settling in, but he could see well enough to know that Glory's car wasn't anywhere around. He'd purposely returned to Luke's after lunch and spent the rest of the afternoon there to give her a chance to finish up and leave for the day. He didn't know how much a saddle that might have been made by her grandfather—and had possibly belonged to her—meant to her, so he wasn't ready to approach her about it. Not yet. Either way, he wouldn't mind being the owner of an Abe Gardner saddle. But he would damn sure find out what was going on as soon as he could.

The smell of fresh paint hit him when he opened the door and stepped inside the kitchen, but it didn't bother him. He was getting used to it. In spite of the disaster that surrounded him, he suspected it wouldn't be long before everything was finished and Glory would be gone. Oh, he'd see her in town, now and then, but not almost every day the way he did now. To tell the truth, he'd grown accustomed to having her there. Even at night when she wasn't there, something about the house felt different. He tried not to think about it or if he'd miss her when she was gone, but sometimes it wasn't that easy.

Without turning on a light, he made his way into the dining room and up the stairs to what was now his bedroom. He hadn't planned to spend much time there. The memory of almost kissing her on the very bed he was now sitting on was something he didn't need. But since the rest of the house was either without furniture or covered in sheets, it was the only place to go. Except for the dining room—and it was filled with everything Glory.

Propping the pillows against the padded headboard, he pulled his cell phone from his pocket and leaned back. He had questions, and he felt pretty sure his sister had the answers.

But after hitting the button that would dial his sister's number, he was rewarded with her voice mail. He left a message.

"If you're crazy enough to think our conversation this afternoon was over, Erin, you're wrong," he said. "And don't think you can avoid me. I'll hunt you down, if that's what it takes."

He'd tossed his hat aside, kicked off his boots and was pulling off his shirt when his phone rang. A quick glance told him his sister hadn't wasted much time.

"I hope you're ready to talk," he said, in greeting.

"Why wouldn't I be?"

He didn't miss the attitude in her voice, and he wasn't going to let her get away with it. "You changed the subject when I asked about the saddle."

"I was dealing with some other things at the time. So sue me."

"You're changing the subject again."

"Not on purpose." When he didn't respond, she sighed. "What is it that you want to know?" she asked with a tone of reluctant surrender in her voice.

Straightforward was his best course, so he repeated the question he'd asked her earlier. "Did you buy a saddle made by Abe Caldwell?"

There was a short silence. "Yes, as a matter of fact I did. And it's a real nice saddle. Well worth what I paid for it."

He didn't care how much she paid or how good the deal was. Not at that moment, anyway. "Who sold it to you?"

"His granddaughter."

"Glory?"

"Well, as far as I know, that's the only granddaughter he had."

"Right. So how did this transaction between you and Glory happen?"

Erin's sigh was loud and clear over the phone. "We ran into each other in Texas. Did you know her mother divorced Glory's daddy and lives there now?"

"Seems I heard something about them splitting, some years ago."

"I never did like that man," Erin said with a sniff. "There was something about him."

Dylan couldn't say he was fond of the man, either, but he hadn't really known him. Besides, none of that mattered, and Erin knew it. She was stalling. "Let's get back to the saddle, Erin."

"Oh, yeah. Well, I happened to meet up with Glory by chance at a barbecue out near Waco, and we got to talking. I mentioned how I'd always wanted a saddle made by her grandfather, but never was lucky enough to have one, and she said she'd sell me hers."

"She just sold it to you, like that?"

"Yeah."

"Why would she do that?"

There was a short silence on the other end before Erin answered. "Apparently she needed some money for something."

Trying hard to ignore the way his stomach tightened, he asked, "Something?"

"Yeah."

He knew better than to lose his temper with Erin. She'd clam up and not tell him anything. But he was going to get the information he wanted from her, come hell or high water. "Do you know what that something was?"

"I know what she told me it was for."

His patience was wearing even thinner. "Erin—"

"She wanted to start a decorating business."

"And I'll bet our best bull that you sent her here to help her out."

"Somebody needed to do something, and not just for her. That house—"

"Okay, okay." His sister had a point, and it was a reminder that she had a soft spot that she kept hidden. She'd do whatever was necessary to keep anyone from discovering it. But he wasn't satisfied with her answer yet.

"I know her marriage to Kyle ended," he said, hoping Erin would understand that he wasn't trying to get information from her that would hurt someone. "She should've had plenty of money from that. Why didn't she have enough to start her business? What kind of start-up would she need? She's using that building that belongs to her grandmother, so—"

"I'm only going to tell you what I know and ask that you don't do or say anything that would hurt her," Erin said. "Do I have your promise?"

He had a bad feeling he wasn't going to like what she had to say. "Yeah, I promise."

Another brief silence had him wondering if they'd lost the connection, but Erin finally spoke. "Her grandmother was about to lose the building. Something about back taxes. I don't know. And the money from her divorce? She used it to pay for her college degree, something that father of hers would never allow her to get. If you want to know anything else, you'll have to ask her."

"I don't need to know anything else." It was true. He didn't. Like his sister, Glory had the same big heart she'd always had, in spite of what he now believed wasn't the charmed life they'd all thought she'd had.

"Dylan, there's something else you need to know. She was relieved to sell that saddle to someone that she knew cared. That saddle is one of the last connections she has to her grandpa, and I think it broke her heart to have to sell. But you keep that to yourself, you hear?"

His fingers tightened on his phone. "I will. And, Erin?"

"Yeah?"

"She's doing a great job with this house."

He could almost hear her smile before she answered. "I never doubted it."

Chapter Six

"How's it going?"

Glory looked up from the papers spread on the dining table that was back in its proper place, surprised to see Dylan so early in the day and standing in the doorway. She hadn't expected to start the new workweek by encountering her client, and it rattled her a little.

"I'm hoping the kitchen will be ready for the appliances by next week." Her heart raced as her gaze met his, and she quickly looked down at the papers again, pretending to be studying them.

"Give me a few hours' notice when you're ready for them, and Luke and I will bring them up from the machine shed and hook them up."

That caused her to look up again. "But I told you—"

"We'll take care of it. It's not like it takes a rocket scientist to plug in a refrigerator and stove."

"There's an ice maker with the refrigerator," she warned, "and a dishwasher, too."

He shook his head and sighed. "You could have a little faith in us."

If she refused to accept the offer, he might take it as an insult, so she simply nodded. "Whatever you say."

"What about the other rooms upstairs?"

"They're coming along. I haven't done a lot with

them, just freshened them up a little," she admitted. But now she wondered if that was enough. "Unless you want something special done with them," she hurried to add. When he continued to watch her, without saying anything, she felt the childish need to squirm. Wishing he would leave so she could relax, she said, "Is there anything else?"

"You really like doing this, don't you?"

His question seemed to come from nowhere, and she wasn't sure what he was asking. "The decorating? I've always enjoyed working with color and fabrics and whole rooms of things, yes."

"You're good at it, you know."

Blinking, she had no doubt her embarrassment was showing, considering how hot her face had become. In fact, she felt warm from head to toe. "Thank you."

After a quick nod, he disappeared, and she sank to a nearby chair, convinced that if he'd stayed another second, her knees would have given out in front of him.

She stared at the doorway, now empty, and wondered what had prompted not only his visit but his questions and interest, whether real or pretend. There were still a few weeks left of work, although most of the major things were done. She wondered how she was going to guard her heart, until her job was finished. Her feelings for Dylan had progressed past simple attraction and she was worried. Relationships weren't high on her list. Making a success of her new business came first. When it came to love, she didn't trust her choices, afraid she would once again put aside her own wants and needs for someone else's.

Too confused by her own feelings, she decided she needed to get busy and forget about Dylan. There was one last bedroom yet to begin work on, and the time seemed perfect for doing just that. Grabbing a notebook of ideas and fabric swatches, plus a pad for sketching, she went upstairs. It was only when she heard the sound of the door on the screened porch downstairs opening and closing several minutes later that she felt safe. She walked across the room to the window in time to see Dylan climbing into his brother's pickup, which then headed down the drive and onto the road. Now she could relax.

She had no idea what to do with the last of the four bedrooms. Standing in the middle of it, the old wallpaper stripped and gone, she tried to imagine a design that was general, yet pleasing and a little different. Nothing came to mind.

Ready to give up and hope for inspiration later, she glanced out one of the tall windows. White, puffy clouds that reminded her of whipped cream drifted in a bright blue sky. The view provided a peaceful feeling. If she could duplicate—

That was it. Exactly what she needed. She'd paint the walls blue and add those plump and billowy clouds. For nighttime, she'd add stars on the ceiling that would glow in the dark.

Half an hour later, sitting on the floor where she could see out the window, she finished sketching. She felt proud. It had been her idea, and she'd done it on her own, without help from a decorating magazine or book.

Energized, now that she knew what she would do, she moved the boxes that held items from the room. She couldn't tell for sure, but she thought it might have been Erin's at one time, although it was difficult to know for sure without asking.

After opening the closet door, she pulled a chair over and climbed up to double-check the shelf at the top to make sure nothing had been left. To her surprise, there was a box that had been pushed to the back corner of the shelf, almost out of her reach. Moving the chair a few inches farther inside, she was able to hook her fingers on the edge of the box and pull it toward her.

She'd just brought the box down and was stepping carefully off the chair when her phone rang. The number was unfamiliar, but the exchange was local.

"Hi, Glory. It's Kate. I hope I'm not bothering you."

"No, of course not," Glory answered, moving the box aside with her foot.

"Good. I called to find out if you've given any more thought to your basket for the box social."

Glory didn't want to admit that she hadn't given it any thought. "Not a lot," she said. "But I do have one question."

"Shoot."

Smiling at Kate's directness, she eased down to the floor. "If it's called a box social, where do the boxes come in?"

"You have a point," Kate answered with a laugh. "I suppose we simply got into the habit of using baskets, since it's held in the park, and most people stay to share what's more a picnic supper than anything. Does that make sense?"

"Perfect sense. Do you think it would be okay if I used a box, though?"

"I don't know why not. Do you have an idea for decorating it?"

Glory smiled again. "You know, I think I just might."

"And you know what you'll be packing in it?"

"Other than your famous double chocolate coconut cake? I decided to keep it simple and do sub sandwiches and potato salad. I'll throw in some chips and pickles for good measure. I don't think I can ruin any of that."

"Oh, Glory, I'm sure your cooking isn't that bad."

"Don't bet on it," Glory replied.

"If you say so, but it couldn't be worse than Trish's was, and we made a cook out of her. It took some time, but, well, she never poisoned anybody."

"That's definitely a blessing," Glory agreed, laughing.

"Then I guess you don't need my help," Kate said. "Except for the cake, and you can either pick it up at my place Friday night, or I'll be happy to bring it to you on Saturday morning when I take my baked goods to the café."

Glory thought about it. "It doesn't matter, as long as nobody knows."

"All right. We'll talk later. And let me know if you need any help."

Glory assured her she would, ended the call and placed the phone on the floor next to her. Curious about what might be in the box she'd found in the closet, she pulled it in front of her. Inside, she found a few pictures of a horse and several hardcover books with a year stamped in gold on the front. She remembered having the same type of books and knew they were probably journals. Aware that they really weren't any of her business, she pulled the top two out to check the dates on them, noting the years were when they'd all been in high school.

As she returned them to the box and moved it out of the way, she heard someone coming up the stairs. "I'm in here," she called, scrambling to her feet.

She heard more footsteps running, followed by the

sound of young male voices, and she smiled. Her help had arrived.

"I'll tell her," one of them said.

"No, it's my turn," came the answer of another.

"Be quiet. She'll hear us."

Laughing quietly, she called out to them. "I've already heard you."

Stu was the first to enter the room. "Ned asked if we could help him start putting up the cabinets. Is that okay?"

"Or did you have something you wanted us to do for you?" Mark asked.

She thought of the supplies she would need for the blue sky and clouds. "I think helping Ned would be a good idea while I run some errands in town. Maybe after that we can get these walls ready to paint."

"I'll help," Mark said before Stu even had the chance.

"You both can, but later," she said, hoping to keep the peace between them.

"Are you going to the box social Saturday?" Stu asked, while she began to gather her drawings.

"Probably," she answered.

"Will you have a basket in the bidding?" Mark asked.

"I'm not—" She saw Dylan standing in the doorway behind the two boys.

"Go ahead and answer his question," he said when she didn't finish her sentence. "We're all curious."

Glory lifted her chin and turned away from them. "I'm not telling whether I've made up my mind to have one or not."

"I guess that's that, boys," Dylan said. "Ned was downstairs asking if I'd seen you. I think he could use a hand with the cabinets."

"Go on," Glory said, turning back around. "We'll work in here later."

Neither of the boys made a move to leave, until Dylan cleared his throat. Within seconds, the boys were going down the long staircase. "I told you how it would be with those boys," he said.

"And I said it wouldn't be a problem," she answered, and walked to the corner where she'd put the box she'd found.

"What's that?" he asked, walking toward her when she picked it up.

"I found it pushed back on the shelf in the closet. I'm not sure who it belongs to."

Dylan pulled the flaps open and peered inside. "It's Erin's stuff. That's her horse, and I remember those books. Diaries, I think."

When he reached in as if to pull one out, Glory cried out. "Don't you dare!" Taking a deep breath, she said, "If they're Erin's, I'm sure she wouldn't want you poking your nose in them. I'll take them and give them to her the next time I see her."

He shrugged his shoulders. "Whatever you say." But instead of leaving or even moving away, he stood looking at her.

"Was there something else?" she asked, wishing he'd leave.

"You didn't answer their question."

"Whose question?"

"Those boys'. Are you going to have a basket at the box social?"

She knew she could simply repeat what she'd told the boys, but she had a better and more truthful answer to give him. "No, I'm not."

From the tiny flicker in his eyes, she had a feeling

her answer had meant something. She just wasn't sure what it was.

"Don't lead those boys on," he said before turning and walking out of the room.

It irritated her that he thought she was doing anything of the kind, but he was gone before she could find her voice, and she was left wondering what was happening. With him. And with her.

NOT AT ALL sure why he was even there, Dylan watched his friends weave their way among the decorated baskets lined up on picnic tables beneath the largest covered shelter in the park.

"What about this one, Dusty?" Morgan called from the far end of a table.

Dusty shook his head. "I've already checked those."

Dylan shook his head at the sight of a grown man sniffing his way up one row of tables, then down another. Dusty had always been his own man, doing whatever he wanted, no matter what other people might think, and Dylan often found himself admiring him for that. But this had him dumbfounded.

"What's with the sniffing?" Dylan asked when Dusty joined him.

"Trying to figure out which one belongs to my wife."

Dylan couldn't believe that Dusty's wife would keep that from him. "You're kidding."

Tipping his cowboy hat back a little farther on his head, Dusty grunted. "Nope. Since I pulled a fast one on Kate back before we were married, she won't even give me a hint. Says I should know by now which one is hers."

Eyeing the rows of baskets, Dylan couldn't imagine

how anyone could pick one out of so many. "Do you? Know which is hers, I mean."

Dusty chuckled. "Oh, she thinks she's tricky, but I'd know her fried chicken anywhere. Trish once told me what ingredients Kate uses, and that's all I needed."

"That's pretty amazing."

"Not as amazing as it tastes. So you're going to bid this year, aren't you? There's some dee-licious stuff in some of those baskets."

Dylan shook his head. "I think I'll pass."

Dusty stepped away, giving him a long look. "Only a fool would pass up an opportunity for one of these homemade meals. Come on, Dylan. Give it a try. I can promise, you won't be disappointed. These ladies try to outdo each other every year."

"You're sure about that," Dylan said, skeptical.

"I guaran-damn-tee it."

Out of the corner of his eye, Dylan saw two of the three boys that Glory had hired as they approached the tables. "I bet I can find it," the first one said to the other.

"Well, it isn't that one," the second one replied.

"Okay, Brent, which one is it, then?"

"Why should I tell you?"

The boys turned, walking farther down the row of tables, and Dylan couldn't hear the answer, which was just as well. Why would he be interested in what a couple of teenagers who happened to have a huge crush on Glory were doing?

Looking around in the opposite direction and wondering where Dusty had gone, he saw Morgan walking his way and waited for the sheriff to join him.

"I don't recall having seen you here before," Morgan said, stopping beside him as they gazed down on the rows of baskets.

"My first time," Dylan answered.

"Then you're bidding?"

Dylan considered it. He'd never come into town for the box social, although he was aware it was held each year to raise money for "municipal improvements," whatever those were. He'd always been too busy to bother. Or maybe it was because he'd made sure he was too busy. Just one more thing to blame on Glory. Something about her being around had made him curious about a lot of things.

"I'll see how it goes," he answered.

"Don't wait too long," Morgan said as more people started filling the area. "You don't want to miss out."

Dylan looked at him. "So you know which one is Trish's?"

Morgan winked. "Sorry, I can't reveal that information."

Dylan shook his head. "So no help for the novice, huh?"

Morgan waved at someone, but when Dylan turned to see whom it was, all he could see was the crowd growing bigger.

"I'll be happy to give you some pointers," Morgan said. "But I need to take care of a couple of things first. I can still give you a quick one to think about."

"Yeah. Sure."

"If you aren't looking for a specific basket, then look for one that's different."

"Different, huh?"

Nodding, Morgan put a hand on his shoulder. "You'll get the hang of it."

"I'll keep that in mind."

After a friendly pat on the back, Morgan assured him he'd find him before the bidding started and walked away whistling. Dylan wondered what he'd gotten himself into. But it seemed he was in, whether he'd planned or even wanted to be or not. He couldn't very well back out now.

Finding an empty spot at a nearby picnic table, he sat on the bench to wait. He had a clear view of the shelter and the gazebo, where the actual bidding would take place. The microphones and speakers were being set up now, so it wouldn't be long until the social got under way.

He tried not to look for Glory, but nothing seemed to work. That disgusted him a little. He wasn't a teenager with raging hormones. But if he was honest with himself, he'd admit that being a teenager had nothing to do with it. He'd been experiencing the grown-up version of those raging hormones lately, in spite of insisting he wasn't interested.

Frowning, he began to wish he'd stayed home. Glory had managed to walk into his life and turn it upside down, even though it was the last thing he wanted. There were now things he thought about that he'd never considered before. Long ago, he'd made the decision to make the ranch his life. That was what his parents would have wanted. Besides, he owed them that and more. It was his penance for a foolish teenage choice that had changed everything. He could never undo that, so he could never undo the decision he'd made. Somehow he'd convinced himself that all that made the loss a little easier. It didn't.

As the crowd moved closer to the large gazebo in the center of the park, he heard someone call his name and looked around.

"Come on," Dusty said, waving at him from what

Dylan guessed must be a prime location. "They're ready to start."

After making his way to where Dusty and Morgan waited, he joined his friends, just as bidding on the first basket began.

"Have you picked one?" Dusty asked.

"Not yet," Dylan answered, wondering what difference it would make.

"Then start looking," Morgan said.

Dylan nodded, and then turned to look around at the crowd. Surprised to see Brent and Mark behind him, he noticed they were craning their necks to see the baskets on the tables. With a silent snort, he went back to watching the bidding.

"You see that box over there?" he heard one of the boys say to the other.

"No."

"Second row, third from the left."

"The one that looks like it's wrapped in a pair of old blue jeans?"

"Yeah, that's the one."

"Yeah, I see it. You think that's hers?"

"I know it is. I saw her talking to Kate McPherson earlier, and that was what she was carrying."

Certain that they were talking about Glory, Dylan had to crane his neck to see around one of the shelter supports to find the box they were talking about. Sure enough, it was wrapped in denim, with a red bandanna tied in a bow on top. And hadn't Morgan told him that if he didn't have a particular basket to bid on, he should find one that was different and vote on it? But did he really want to win Glory's basket?

Fifteen minutes later, the denim-covered box was handed to silver-haired City Councilman Mike Stacy, a professional auctioneer. "Smells pretty darn good," he said, turning it around. "And it's mighty nice-looking, too. So who wants to open up the bidding on this masterpiece?"

"Five dollars," someone on the other side of the gazebo shouted.

Councilman Stacy pointed in that direction. "Five dollars—do I hear six?"

"You're really sure?" the second boy asked from behind Dylan.

"Totally. Now, how much do we want to bid?"

"Six!" the other shouted, instead of answering.

Dylan wanted to turn around and tell them that bidding on her basket, if it was her basket, wasn't going to help them much where Glory was concerned. But he didn't want to hurt them, so he kept quiet.

By the time the bid went to fifteen dollars, Dylan was feeling a little uncomfortable, and the boys just kept bidding.

"Sixteen!" he called out before realizing what he'd done.

Dusty slapped him on the back. "There ya go. I knew you'd pick it up. It's just like bidding on a prize heifer."

The next thing Dylan knew, the bid went up another half-dollar.

"Don't give up now," Morgan said, from his other side.

Dylan stuck with it, until he won the bid at twenty dollars. He hoped it was worth it.

Councilman Stacy held the basket high. "Would the little lady who this belongs to please step up to join this gentleman for supper?"

Dylan turned to look at Dusty. "What? What's going on? What does that mean?"

Dusty glanced at Morgan and shrugged. "Nobody told you?"

The crowd began to part, and Dylan began to panic. "Told me what?"

"The bidder gets to share the contents with the woman who made the basket."

Dylan watched as the crowd moved to reveal the owner. Stepping out and passing the other bidders and basket makers, Glory raised her hand. "It's my basket," she announced, and glanced at Dylan.

When he saw the hesitancy in her eyes, he wondered why, but he also wondered if Dusty and Morgan had encouraged him to bid on purpose. Of course, it wasn't their fault. He'd listened to the boys and let the thrill of competition get the best of him. If only he'd known he'd been bidding to share the contents with her. He could only hope he was ready for this, because he couldn't think of a way out. The crazy thing about it was that he wasn't sure he wanted to.

GLORY REALIZED SHE'D just cleared her throat for the third time in less than five minutes. What was it that made her so nervous? She'd been around Dylan nearly every day for almost a month, so there was no reason to feel nervous around him. They were friends. Or at least that was what she kept telling herself every time he stepped into the room and she found herself feeling like a teenager with a crush. It was crazy.

"Looks good," he said.

Her hands trembled as she pulled out the container of potato salad and set it on the picnic table. "I hope it's worth your bid. I haven't done a lot of cooking."

"Neither have I."

Sure he was laughing at her, she looked up and

straight into his green eyes. That simple act chased every thought from her mind.

"Here, let me help."

His voice jerked her back to reality, and she tried to get a grip on herself. "Thank you."

Neither of them spoke again as they placed the food, plates and utensils on the table. When they were done, he leaned back and looked at the table. "I think I got a good deal on this box-social thing."

A nervous giggle bubbled inside her, but she kept it from escaping. "We'll see if you still think so after you've tasted everything."

She felt his gaze on her when he replied. "I'm not scared."

"Maybe you should be."

Picking up his plate, she filled it, while he uncorked the bottle of wine she'd added to the basket at the last minute.

"You don't mind?" he asked, indicating the bottle in his hands, when she looked up.

"That's up to you," she answered with a shrug. But somehow she felt she could trust him. "Really, it's okay with me."

She watched as he poured wine into two glasses, while her thoughts chased around in her head. Feeling she should at least give him some sort of explanation of her reaction at finding the box of bottles, she took a deep breath. "I'm sorry about the way I reacted that day. It isn't any of my business. But my father sometimes drank too much, although not all the time. And Kyle—"

"He could drink everybody in the class under the table."

Nodding, she thought about how Kyle would come home, reeking of bourbon and perfume, and she never said a word. She'd been the good little wife, just as she'd been the good little daughter. And she'd never been happy. Now, for the first time that she could remember, she was discovering what it was like to enjoy life without the fear of doing or saying the wrong thing.

"So, what do you do for fun?" she asked.

"Ranching doesn't leave much time for fun."

She noticed that he didn't look at her when he answered, and she wondered why. "Are you saying that work is your fun?"

He still avoided looking at her. "Luke and I have been busy making a success of the ranch. There hasn't been a lot of free time."

"Everybody needs to get away, no matter how important your work is. But you're saying no vacations, no trying something new, just for the fun of it?"

He looked up and straight into her eyes. "If I said that, I'd be lying."

"Aha! So spill," she teased. "I swear I won't tell a soul."

"Never thought you would."

When he didn't continue, she hoped a little verbal nudge would get him talking. "So what is it you do?"

He took a drink of wine, then pushed the glass away. "Every year in the spring, I take a trip somewhere and try something new."

Propping her elbows on the table, she watched him, pleased that she'd dragged something out of him and eager to learn more. "In the spring? Like in May?"

"Late May."

She knew exactly when and was reminded again of the change in him after the accident that had killed his parents. "Is there a place you like better than others?"

He tipped his head back and closed his eyes. "The mountains. And I like the ocean, too. It just depends."

"On what?"

"On what I want to do."

"Such as?"

He stood and untangled his long legs from the bench of the picnic table. "You sure do ask a lot of questions."

"I—" She sensed something in him that she couldn't define. What could it be that he did every year that he wouldn't share with her? A lot of things immediately came to mind, but none of them were anything she thought Dylan would do or even want to do. At least not the Dylan she remembered.

"You know," she said, thinking out loud, "you may think I don't remember you that much from school, but I do." When he didn't say anything, she continued. "You were one of the nice boys. I never once heard you bully anyone. In fact, I once saw you stand up for Danny Johnson when Kyle and some of the others were giving him a hard time."

"I don't remember that."

She suspected he did, but it was obvious that he didn't want to talk about it. Giving up on trying to get him to talk to her, she stood, ready to end their lovely picnic and call it a day.

"I've been white-water rafting," he announced.

Her hands stilled, and she looked up from clearing the table. "Really?"

He nodded. "Yeah. And rock climbing."

"Oh, Dylan, that's so— Isn't it scary? I mean, hanging on the side of a mountain or whatever?"

He met her gaze. "I like parasailing a lot, too."

She couldn't believe what he was saying. "Are you telling me you've really done all those things?"

"Yeah, all of them. And more."

There was only one more question she needed to ask. "Why?"

He shrugged and looked off in the distance. "I don't know. Maybe because it's so different than ranching. Or maybe it's because I can."

"You're a risk taker, then," she said. "Is that it?"

"Maybe. I don't think about it. I just do it."

"Tempting fate? Isn't that kind of, well, crazy?"

"I guess I don't see it that way. I enjoy doing those things. It's exhilarating."

And dangerous. But he already knew that, so she didn't bother to point it out.

He helped her pack the last of the things into the box, and then they stood, looking at each other. "You're a pretty good cook, you know that?"

She smiled at the compliment. "With a little practice, I might get better."

"I'm glad it was your box I bid on. I had a real nice time."

She hoped he wasn't just trying to be polite, but before she could worry about it, she felt him move closer. Looking up, she realized what was about to happen, and she couldn't have stopped him if she'd wanted to.

His lips touched hers, tentatively, sweetly, lingering for a moment. And then the kiss was over. She nearly died. She wanted more. She knew it was wrong. Very wrong. But that didn't keep her from wanting.

Chapter Seven

He never should have kissed her.

Dylan leaned back against the south side of the barn, waiting for the big stock tank to fill with water, and tried to focus on his most recent white-water canoeing trip. It had been the most exciting—and dangerous—thing he'd tried yet. At one point, he'd nearly lost his canoe when a sudden shift in the flow of water took him over a waterfall. He'd honestly thought he'd be taking his last breath, but somehow he'd managed to survive. Trying to run it through his mind again to feel the exhilaration and total fear wasn't working as well as he'd hoped. The image of Glory's sweet face, tipped up to his, kept taking over. "Damn," he muttered, shaking his head. This had to stop. He'd rather ride that rapid again ten times than let himself fall for someone, especially Glory.

It wasn't as if he'd planned to kiss her or given it any thought in advance. It had just happened. He couldn't have stopped himself from doing it, if he'd even considered it. He hadn't. He was in the middle of it before he realized what he was doing. Not knowing how to tell her that he'd enjoyed sharing the box supper with her more than he'd ever enjoyed anything could have been a factor. But if he tried to blame it on that, he'd be lying. The fact was he'd been watching her, thinking of things he shouldn't, and she'd looked up at him with something in her eyes that he couldn't name. Before he knew what was—

"Shouldn't you turn off the water?"

He whipped his head around to see Glory standing at the corner of the barn, while not a foot away from him the tank was overflowing. All he wanted to do at that moment was whack the back of his head against the side of the barn until his common sense returned. He suspected that might not ever happen. He seemed to be losing chunks of that common sense every time she came around.

"Yeah, uh, thanks. I wasn't paying attention," he said. "I'll have to turn it off in the barn."

"You're probably wondering why I'm here to bother you again," she said as he started for the barn entrance.

Not having a clue how to reply, he kept silent and entered the barn. Reaching the faucet, he turned it off, and realized she'd followed him inside. "You're not bothering me. You pointed out that I wasn't paying attention. No telling how long I'd have stood there with water pouring over my boots."

To his surprise, she laughed. "It wasn't that bad. But your mind was definitely not on the tank."

No, it was on you. Not that he could admit it to her. He didn't even like admitting it to himself.

He looked up when he heard her clear her throat.

"If you have the time…" she said, without looking at him directly, "there's something I'd like to show you. If you can spare a few minutes."

Other than some disaster, he could think of only one thing she could want to show him. "Is my office done?" he asked. She'd asked him to stay away from what used to be his bedroom while it was being worked on, and his curiosity had gotten to the point that his patience was wearing thin.

She shook her head. "Not quite. But soon."

"Right." *Soon* was the answer she gave the most often when asked about the progress of his house.

Her smile was tentative at first, and she ducked her head for a moment before turning to walk out of the barn. "This one is different. I think you'll be surprised," she said over her shoulder when he followed.

He didn't doubt he would be. She'd been nothing but surprises since walking into his house that first morning. But that was not what he needed to be thinking about. "So what's left to do?" he asked.

"Do? Oh, you mean with the house. Other than your office and the kitchen, which may be ready later today, the living room needs some finishing touches, new paint in the dining room—which won't take long—and the last bedroom."

For a second, he couldn't take a breath. The changes and decorating would be done soon. Glory would collect her pay and leave. He wouldn't see her unless it was in town. Wasn't that a good thing?

His chest tightened when he realized he didn't want her to just disappear from his life. But she would. Even if she didn't, there wasn't anything he could offer her. His life was the ranch. That was what he'd chosen.

She was nearly at the house by the time he caught up with her. Reaching around her as she stepped up on the first step, he opened the old screen door and once again felt the loss of his parents. Losing someone and the pain it left was not something he wanted to experience again. Not only had he made the wrong choice when he didn't go straight home the afternoon of the storm, but he'd never realized his grief would affect so many things in his life.

"Upstairs," she said, walking through the kitchen and into the dining room.

Only a few steps behind her, he followed her up the stairs. "What's left up here?"

"The last bedroom," she answered, reaching the top. "I want to know what you think of what I've been working on."

"I don't know anything about decorating," he insisted. "I don't know how I can help."

At the door of the last of the four rooms, she stopped. "I did something a little different. I just want to be sure it's all right."

Shrugging, he followed her into the room, and immediately saw what she'd done. "Are those clouds?" he asked, looking around.

"You could tell!" she said from behind him.

He faced her and wondered how she could have been worried. "Well, yeah. It's pretty obvious."

"What's obvious?"

They both turned toward the door.

"Wow," Luke said. "This is unbelievable." He grinned at Glory. "In a good way."

"Then you like it?"

"Who wouldn't? Dylan, you like it, don't you?" Luke asked.

Dylan nodded, wondering how either of them could think he didn't. "I'm blown away."

Glory's previously uncertain smile widened. "I thought it was something anyone would be comfortable with, but I was really thinking of Brayden, Luke. I could imagine him staring up at the clouds."

"Oh, he'd love it. We need to hire you to do something like this for him at our place."

"Good idea," Dylan said before Glory could think of a reason to say no.

She pointed to the ceiling. "The stars up there glow in the dark."

Dylan was amazed that she thought of little things like that. He'd never expected her to do the thorough job she'd done. Some fresh paint and a few other things were all he'd imagined. She'd definitely gone above and beyond.

"When the boys get here tomorrow, I'll have them move the furniture back in," she said, walking toward the door. Looking back, she stopped. "Wait—I forgot to take that box of Erin's things with me," she said.

"I'll get it," Dylan said.

She hurried to the corner of the room. "We already went over this, remember?" She picked up the box and held it close. "I'll take it and give it to her the next time I see her."

"She thinks I'll read Erin's old diaries," he explained to Luke.

Luke grunted. "As if there was anything in there except stuff about her horse."

"Right." Dylan glanced at Glory.

"You probably *would* snoop," she said with a sniff.

"You're wrong, but okay, you can take care of the box."

She stopped at the door. "I think I hear Ned in the kitchen. Maybe you should check to see if he's ready for the appliances."

"Are you staying around?" Dylan asked.

Stepping outside into the hall, she looked back and

shook her head. "No, I have some work to do at the shop today."

When Glory was gone, Luke turned to Dylan. "I guess my timing was good. I told Hayley I was hoping we'd get a chance to finish the kitchen today."

"I'm ready if you are. Lead the way."

Luke had been right. When they reached the kitchen, the carpenter was standing back and admiring his work. "Looks good, don't you think?" he asked the brothers.

"It does," Dylan agreed. "Nothing like it was before, that's for sure." It was almost as if it was a completely new room. After seeing what Glory had done with his bedroom and the cloud bedroom, he was eager to see how the kitchen would look when they were done.

"It's ready for the appliances?" Luke asked Ned.

"Sure is. I'll stick around to give you a hand."

"Getting the appliances loaded in the back of a truck is going to be a trick," Dylan said, thinking of the size of the refrigerator.

"We'll get it done," Luke assured him.

Two hours and several trips later, his muscles aching, Dylan stood with Luke in the kitchen. "I never imagined anything like this," he admitted.

"She does a damn fine job," Luke said, leaning back against the doorframe that opened into the new hallway. "I never realized she was so talented."

"Erin didn't doubt it."

"Maybe you should do something about it."

Dylan looked at him. "About Erin?"

"Your head is thicker than I thought." Luke straightened and started for the door, but turned back. "Don't screw this up."

The last thing Dylan wanted his brother to know was that he'd formed an attraction to Glory. If that was what it was called. "There's nothing to screw up," he answered, hoping that would be the end of it.

Luke nodded. "Yeah, and pigs fly."

"You're imagining things," Dylan answered, but Luke was already out the door and headed for his truck.

With a sigh, he looked around the room that Glory had designed. "It's great," he said to no one. "Now what?"

GLORY PULLED A plate out of the plastic dish drainer and began drying it, while her grandmother scrubbed a serving dish from supper. She never would have thought she would enjoy washing and drying dishes, but since returning to Desperation and moving in with her grandmother, she'd discovered that not only was it somehow relaxing, but she enjoyed the talk they shared while working.

"You haven't seen my dad back in town, have you?"

Louise's hands stilled in the water, and she turned her head to look at Glory. "Seems no one in Desperation has seen hide nor hair of him."

Nodding, Glory stared at the rim of the plate in her hand. "I guess that's a good sign. I had a feeling that once Mom left, he'd move on. He never struck me as someone who really enjoyed living here, except for the attention."

The tick-tock of the old clock on the wall could be heard in the silence as Louise took her hands from the sink and dried them on her apron. She didn't immediately look at Glory, but when she finally did, her eyes were filled with contrition. "There were things I did and didn't do when you were growing up that I thought at the time were right, but they weren't."

Glory put the plate on the countertop. "It didn't have anything to do with you."

Louise sighed. "It did. I should have found a way to stop your mama from marrying him, but Sherry has always had a stubborn streak." Sucking in her bottom lip, she closed her eyes. "Maybe it's time we talk about all of it."

She took her grandmother's hands in hers. "I don't mind if you don't want to talk about it. I was only wondering—"

"We'll talk about it," Louise said with a decisive nod. "I want to. There are things that have been left unsaid for too long." She untied her apron and pulled it off. Then she moved to the well-used kitchen table and pulled out a chair. "Sit," she said, and took her usual place.

Glory did as she was told and settled on the chair to her grandmother's right. Feeling as if she'd just opened Pandora's box, she thought an explanation for why she asked about her father might be in order. "I never understood my dad when I was growing up, but I think I'm finally beginning to, thanks to the time I spent in Texas with my mom."

Louise nodded again. "I'm glad for that. The two of you needed to make your peace." Tears glittered in her eyes. "I only wished I could have…"

Placing her hand on her grandmother's, Glory shook her head. "This is too hard for you, Gram."

Her grandmother's blue-eyed gaze changed to steel when she turned her head to look at her. "No harder than it was for you to grow up with the father you had."

Glory felt the old ache. When she tried to pull her hand away, her grandmother clasped her fingers around it. "I don't think—"

"I should have stepped in when I started suspecting that although Glen might have been a good husband, he was a devil when it came to anyone else, especially you."

Glory shook her head. "It wasn't that bad—"

"Don't you stand up for him! He doesn't deserve it."

Glory dared to meet her grandmother's gaze. "I did all right. It could have been worse—much worse—but it wasn't."

Louise leaned forward. "Your mother didn't do anything about it, did she?"

"No."

"But she knew."

Fear and relief fought for release, but Glory couldn't speak, so she nodded.

Squeezing Glory's hand, Louise sighed. "I never thought he was the kind of father he should have been. I should have gone to Sherry—"

"She would have told you that you were imagining things." Glory bit her lip, wishing she hadn't spoken. She loved her mother, but she had only just begun to forgive the woman who had not been her ally in the war with her father. "We've talked about it, Gram. Mama and I. She couldn't feel any worse."

"That makes two of us," Louise replied with a heavy sigh. "I only want you to have the best, Glory. That's all that matters to me now."

"Thank you," Glory said in a whisper, and then she smiled. "It wouldn't have been nearly so bad if he'd let me have my art. And a horse. I wanted a horse so much."

This time it was Gram's turn to pat Glory's hand. "And there was no reason to deny you that. He had the money, and if he hadn't, your grandpa and I would have taken care of it."

"He nearly came undone when he found out that Papa made me the saddle." As soon as it was out of Glory's mouth, her eyes began to sting with tears. She couldn't tell her grandmother that she'd sold the one thing that had meant the world to her, but it had been the only way she could raise the money to pay off the back taxes on the shop building. She had no regrets about doing that, but she did miss the one thing that connected her to the best part of her past.

"He hurt you, didn't he?"

Sniffing back the tears, Glory shrugged. "He expected me to be who he wanted me to be, not who I was. And I did what he wanted me to do, believing that a daughter did as she was told. By the time I was a little older, I didn't think about it. He gained attention because I was popular. I understand that now."

A tear slipped down her grandmother's cheek. "I'm so sorry."

"Don't be. I could have told him I didn't want to be a cheerleader or any of the rest, but I didn't. I don't think Mom realized how I felt. She thought I was happy. But it's over. So let's talk about something happy, okay?"

Chuckling, Louise wiped the tear away and then stood. "Let me put the coffee on. It's going to be a long night."

"IT'S HARD TO believe this is the same kitchen where we fought over the sand plum jelly every morning," Luke said, tipping his chair back on two legs.

Dylan frowned at him and set his coffee cup on the table. "Don't let Glory catch you doing that."

Luke's eyes widened, and he settled the chair solidly on all fours. "Dang, Dylan. Can't a guy get a break? Don't tell me you're getting to be a nag."

Dylan grunted. "I just don't want to have to explain

how those marks got on this new floor before the rest of the fixing up is finished."

"A little whipped, are you?"

Luke's smile put Dylan's teeth on edge. "Nope. But there's no sense in upsetting the decorator before the job is done." As he pulled out his chair to sit at the table, he heard the sound of a vehicle turning into the lane. "I wonder who that is. Glory said she wouldn't be here until the afternoon."

Luke stood and walked to the window over the sink. "Looks like our sister's decided to pay us a little visit. When was the last time you heard from her?" he asked over his shoulder.

Dylan joined him and watched the motor home pulling a horse trailer drive past the end of the lane and on around the house. "Not since that day at Lou's when Jeff mentioned Erin had bought that saddle that Abe had made." He didn't say anything about calling their sister later that day. There was no need. "She has a habit of turning up like a bad penny."

Luke snorted and turned to him. "And never with any warning."

"Right." Returning to the table, Dylan sat and reached for his coffee cup. Taking a sip, he felt torn about his sister's sudden and unannounced arrival. On one hand, he wondered if she had Glory's saddle with her. He'd decided to buy it from her, no matter what she wanted for it. On the other, he had to hope she'd lost the ability to read him like a book. She'd know immediately that there was something going on with him, besides the usual. That was the last thing he needed. She'd be like a dog with an old bone and keep after him until he opened up and admitted— What? Even he didn't know what was going on inside him when it came to Glory.

While he tried to wipe all thoughts of Glory from his mind before his sister walked in, Luke joined him at the table. "Do you think she'll be okay with all the changes that have been made?"

Dylan grunted as he listened for his sister to announce her arrival. "Since it was her idea that they needed to be made, but I'm the one paying for it, I can't see why she'd have any reason to complain."

"True, but—"

The screen door on the porch squeaked, followed by the sound of boots stepping inside and the door banging shut. Erin had often said it was as much her house as it was Dylan's, so it was no surprise to him that she didn't bother to knock. It was true that they all shared ownership of the house and the ranch, and Dylan had never thought it a problem until Erin had threatened to sell the house only weeks ago. Because she was the oldest, she had the power, but they'd never butted heads until that night.

"How lucky can a girl get?" she said, standing in the doorway of the kitchen. "Two good-looking guys with coffee. What could possibly be better?"

Luke got to his feet and picked up his petite sister, swinging her around in a circle. "Having a wayward sister home again is better."

Erin laughed and slapped a hand on her cowboy hat when it started to fly off. "And here I thought I was just dizzy from seeing you two. Now put me down."

"It's always a pleasure to have you home." Dylan gestured toward the cabinets when Luke set her on her feet. "Grab yourself a cup and take a load off your feet, big sis."

Planting her hands on her hips, Erin glared at him. "Are you saying I've gained weight?"

He shook his head. "Nope, just trying to rile you so you'll wear out that orneriness you always bring home with you."

The next thing he knew she had her arms around his neck and had pulled him down to give him a noisy kiss on his cheek. "Think that'll help?" she asked.

"Maybe. How long are you planning to stay?"

After letting him go, she gave him a playful shove. "As long as I can irritate you and before I wear out my welcome."

He swallowed his chuckle and shook his head. "Not long, then, I see."

"Okay, you two," Luke said, taking his place at the table again.

"I know I shouldn't say this," she said over her shoulder, while pouring a cup of coffee, "but this place looks fantastic."

"I can't argue with that," Luke said.

Turning around, she looked directly at Dylan. "What about you? What do you think?"

Not wanting her to think it was a big deal to him, he shrugged. "It works."

"It *works?*" Erin sighed and sat on the chair Dylan pushed out for her with his foot. "That's the thanks I get for getting you some help?"

"I didn't ask for any help."

She opened her mouth, obviously ready to argue, and then shut it. Lowering her head to stare into the cup of coffee in front of her, she said, "You're right. You never do."

Luke looked from one to the other and filled the sudden silence in the room. "Why do you two always leave me out of these things?"

Dylan refused to be the one who answered. Erin had

meddled in his life. She'd proven that she hadn't had any faith in him. Not that there had been any reason for her to. Sitting back in his chair, he crossed his arms on his chest and said nothing. She could do the explaining. He only hoped she didn't give all the details.

It took only a moment for her to shake her head and turn to Luke. "I ran into Glory down in Texas when she was living with her mom, and she mentioned she was coming back to Desperation and starting a new business."

Luke glanced at Dylan. "And?"

Erin hesitated for a second. "I hired her to do some decorating here and fix up this place."

"That's it?"

Dylan watched as she shrugged but didn't look directly at Luke. "Pretty much," she answered.

Luke didn't seem to notice her evasion or Dylan's relief. "She's done a terrific job. You should look around, Erin. Right, Dylan?"

She shot to her feet. "Great idea! Where do I start?"

"Upstairs," Dylan answered.

"What about there?" she asked, pointing to the new hallway that had been part of his bedroom.

"Sorry, nobody can go in there."

Erin's eyes narrowed when she turned to look at him. "Nobody?"

"Nobody. Not even me." Dylan pushed away from the table and stood. "I'll take you upstairs and show you around. I think you'll be happy with her work." After he rinsed his coffee cup at the sink, he headed for the dining room and the stairs.

"Dylan?"

He ignored her and kept going. By the time he reached the upstairs landing, he looked back to see her starting up the steps. "This second story is pretty much finished," he told her as she reached the top step. "I'm pretty sure that you're going to like what she did to your old bedroom."

"Dylan, I'm—"

"This is what you wanted, wasn't it?" he asked, turning toward her. "Everything looks different."

She nodded. "But I'm not the one who has to like it."

"Then there's not a problem. I like it." In fact, he hadn't realized how badly he needed the changes. But Glory seemed to have somehow known.

Erin looked around the second-floor hallway. "She definitely does good work."

"I won't argue with that. Do you want to see what else she's done?"

"No. I don't need to right now. I'll take a longer look in the morning," she answered, in an offhanded tone. "Now, why is it you really wanted me to come upstairs?"

He squinted at her through narrowed eyes, wondering how she always knew what he was up to. "I want to buy that saddle."

"I figured you would."

Not sure how she could have known that in advance, he ignored it. "I'll give you what you paid plus ten percent."

"I don't know…" she said, her nose scrunched as if it wasn't a decent offer.

"Twenty percent."

"And if I say no?"

He was losing what little patience he had. "How much do you want for it?"

She named an amount.

"That's all?"

"That's what I paid for it. I never intended to make a profit."

All he could do was stare at her. Somehow, she was always one step ahead of him.

"What are you going to do with it?" she asked. "If I sell it to you."

He shook his head. He'd only thought about how to get it from his sister. "I don't know yet."

Erin put a hand on his arm and smiled. "I'm sure you'll think of something."

He watched her walk down the stairs and felt more confused than ever. They'd fought like cats and dogs as kids, but he'd been her biggest ally and had always looked after her because she was so much smaller than him. Even grown-up, she had to stand on her toes to reach five feet tall. She'd needed someone to watch over her. As far as he was concerned, she still did. But somehow it was always Erin who came through for him when he didn't know he needed someone.

He still hadn't decided what he would do with Glory's saddle, once Erin gave in and sold it to him. He wasn't even sure if he would tell her he had it, and he sure hoped she wouldn't ask Erin about it.

Chapter Eight

Erin settled on the new sofa in the living room and leaned back. "You've done an amazing job, Glory. Not that I expected you wouldn't. But I have to say I was— What is it that people say? Pleasantly surprised? Yeah, that's it. I was pleasantly surprised when I walked into the kitchen yesterday. But that's putting it mildly. It's wonderful."

Embarrassed by the praise, Glory ducked her head. "You have no idea what it means to me to hear that, but also to have the opportunity to do it. I always loved this house from afar, but never dreamed I would be doing what I've done here."

"Everything has gone okay, then?"

"Of course," Glory answered. "Why wouldn't it?"

Erin shrugged. "No reason. But sometimes Dylan can be stubborn." Shifting to face Glory, she smiled. "Like me. But don't tell him I said so."

Glory wasn't sure how much or what she should say, but Erin had been especially nice to her. "He has his moments," she admitted. "And it's hard to get him to talk."

"It has been since— Well, for quite a while. Not that he was chatty before that," Erin rushed to say. "He has the personality of the firstborn, even though he isn't, but maybe because he's the oldest boy. He took on responsibilities that a grown-up would have run from, and he never complained. Not once."

Glory studied her. Erin's face showed how much she cared about both of her brothers. "But he wasn't the only one," she pointed out. "If I remember, you were on the verge of taking off for a serious rodeo career, but you stayed until Luke turned eighteen."

Color flooded Erin's face. "It wasn't a big deal."

"It was to them. Sure, I've heard them complain, but it's plain to see they really care about you. I envy you."

"Thanks." Erin was clearly uncomfortable and immediately changed the subject. "There isn't much left to do, is there?"

Shaking her head, Glory hoped Erin couldn't see how much she dreaded finishing the job. She'd enjoyed the time she'd spent in the Walker home. There was something special about being in a house that was over one hundred years old and had seen generations of a family live their lives in it. In fact, she'd been thinking about a special project she wanted to do as a gift.

But Erin had asked a question, and she deserved a better answer. "The office is finished. I'll show it to Dylan later."

"Can I see it?"

Glory laughed, but shook her head. "Sorry, no. I haven't let him go into it, so it really wouldn't be fair."

Erin's frown was obviously an exaggeration she couldn't hold for long, because she laughed, too. "Oh, all right. So what else is left?"

"There's one room upstairs that I'm close to finishing, the dining room needs some fresh paint and a fantastic accent rug, and there are a few other odds and ends, but then that's it."

"You'll be leaving soon."

Glory tried to smile. "I guess I will."

Erin's expression was pensive, too. "But you'll still be in Desperation, right?"

"Of course!" Glory grinned, still excited to be living in her hometown again. "I know there are people who wish they could get away, but I'm happy to be back again. What about you? You left a long time ago, the same as I did. Do you plan to come back permanently?"

For a moment, Erin didn't speak. "I haven't decided. It's possible."

Glory's interest was piqued. She liked Erin and hoped they could be friends. There were so few of them left in town who weren't married and involved with their families. "Very possible?"

Erin smiled, but gave a half shrug. "That remains to be seen."

"Oh!" Glory cried when she suddenly remembered she'd brought something for Erin.

"What is it?"

"I have something for you. It's in my car." Scrambling from the sofa, she hurried outside and grabbed the box that Dylan had said belonged to his sister.

When she returned, she put the box on the sofa between her and Erin. "I found this in the closet upstairs in the room I guess used to be yours. I was afraid Dylan might get nosy if I left it here, so I took it home."

"Yeah?" Erin opened the cardboard flaps and looked inside. "Oh, good grief," she cried and instantly laughed.

Glory noticed misty tears in her eyes when Erin picked up the photo of the horse. "I didn't go through it. But as soon as I realized those were journals, well, I knew they needed to be guarded from prying eyes."

"I'd forgotten I left these here," Erin said with a sentimental sniff. Looking up with a watery smile, she said, "Thank you for looking out for them."

"Do you think there might be more pictures of your horse in there?"

Erin's smile widened. "Could be. Let's look." She began pulling out the journals and handed them to Glory, but the shift in contents sent the box tipping onto the floor.

"Oh, dear," Glory said. "I'm sorry. Looks like there are some papers—"

"I'll take a look at them later," Erin said, scrambling to gather the spilled papers together and stuffing them back in the box.

The sound of boot heels could be heard in the kitchen, and Glory turned to see whom it was, her heart beating with the anticipation of showing Dylan his new office. She wasn't disappointed.

He stood in the doorway and greeted his sister first. "Hey, Erin." But his attention was on Glory. "I have a few minutes, if it's a good time to take a look at the office."

Erin jumped to her feet. "I'd better get going. I promised to visit some friends in town." Grabbing the box, she hurried to the door where Dylan stood, poked him with a finger and looked back at Glory. "I'll talk to you again before I leave," she said, and disappeared into the kitchen.

Neither Dylan nor Glory spoke until the sound of the screen door closing echoed through the house. Although earlier, Glory had had complete faith in what she'd done with Dylan's office, she was suddenly nervous that he would hate it. Panic gripped her as she thought of all the things he might dislike.

"Uh, Glory?"

She hadn't yet made it to the wallpaper she'd used when she realized he'd spoken. "Maybe another day or two would—"

"I'd like to see it now."

When she tried to swallow and discovered she couldn't, she knew her fear was to blame. She'd never felt afraid that her work wouldn't measure up, so why would she now?

Standing, she drew herself up and squared her shoulders, taking a deep, calming breath. "Then let's take a look, shall we?"

"Sounds good."

He stepped aside when she moved into the kitchen. "I had this short hallway built," she said, "to give you more privacy. It allows visitors access to the bathroom, without having to go through the room. I felt it works better, whether you want to make this room your bedroom or your office."

"I don't have a lot of visitors."

There was a touch of impatience in his voice, so she reached for the doorknob as she looked up and smiled. It was as much to assure herself as him. "Maybe you will someday." She twisted the knob, but stopped. "Would you mind if I make sure everything is ready?"

He lifted one shoulder, but didn't look pleased. "If you need to."

Trying for another smile, she opened the door just wide enough to slip inside, and then she blew out a breath. A quick flip of the light switch bathed the room in a soft glow. Looking around, she was reminded once again of how much she liked the room. It was so Dylan. She only hoped he liked it, too.

"You can come in now." She reached to open the door, hoping for the best.

He stepped inside and stopped, his gaze sweeping across the room quickly, then again more slowly. "I can't believe it."

She held her breath. Was that good or bad?

He turned to look at her. "You're—" He shook his head. "I don't know. Unbelievable."

She dared to let herself breathe, and then smiled, slowly at first, until her face began to hurt. "That's good, right?"

He grunted, while surveying the room again. "The floor looks great, all shiny and new. And the colors... Green and tan and red." He looked at her. "How did you know?"

"These are the colors I see you wear the most," she answered with a shrug, although she was bursting with pride. "Then you like it?"

His chuckle was deep and sent shivers through her. "Yeah," he said. "I like it. And I really like that wallpaper."

The wallpaper had been the first thing she'd found. She'd chosen an outdoor scene with the colors that seemed to define him, and then built the rest of the room around it. The dark, but not too dark wainscoting, the leather wing chair with matching ottoman and the wall of bookcases all tied in with the large desk against one wall. She couldn't have been happier.

"I loved doing it," she admitted.

"It shows."

She looked at him, and her knees weakened. His green eyes had darkened, and it felt as if he could see everything about her, her thoughts, her dreams, her wishes...and her feelings for him.

Quickly clearing her throat, she forced herself to look away and tried to be as professional as possible.

"I'm glad you like it. Making my first client happy was a big deal."

"We need to celebrate."

"Celebrate?"

He nodded. "I was thinking…"

She knew she shouldn't allow it, but her heart beat faster in anticipation. "Yes?"

"Would you like to go riding tomorrow?"

Images of fast cars and motorcycles flashed through her mind. "Riding?"

"I know you used to ride a long time ago, and I thought… We have a real nice mare you might like."

Horses! "I'd love to go riding with you, Dylan." She hoped she didn't sound as though she was gushing, but the thought of riding a horse again excited her beyond words.

"Glory?"

Swallowing her excitement, she looked up.

"You know, I'm going to have to thank my sister for sending you to decorate my house."

Unable to answer, she nodded.

For the third time since he'd saddled the horse he'd chosen for Glory, Dylan checked the cinch. The saddle was an old one that had belonged to his sister, long before she'd left for the rodeo circuit. Erin still hadn't said if she would sell him Glory's saddle. In fact, when he'd asked her earlier that morning, she'd said she was still considering it. He'd been angry that she wouldn't give him an answer, but he dropped the subject, certain she'd come around soon enough.

He suspected she would be leaving soon. Even though she'd said more times than he could count that she'd stop for a real visit, she never stayed more than a day or two. He didn't expect this time would be any different.

He heard a vehicle slow down and pull up front, certain it was Glory. When the sound of a car door slamming shut soon followed, he led the mare and his own horse out of the smaller barn and into the adjacent corral. Just as he'd thought, Glory was approaching the barn and waved when he looked her way.

"Oh, she's beautiful!" she called to him.

Her excitement made his heart beat faster, and he waited until she was closer before he spoke. "She's gentle, but not shy. I think the two of you will get along."

Glory climbed through the wood fence and approached the horses he held. "What's her name?"

"Cinnamon."

"Good choice," she said, reaching up to run her hand down the mare's reddish-brown nose. She looked over her shoulder at him. "I think I could have saddled her myself, but it's probably a good thing you did it for me. It might have taken me a while to get it right. This way we'll have more time to ride."

It was exactly what he'd been thinking when he made the decision to get both horses ready before she arrived, but he didn't want her to think he doubted her experience. "You'd have done fine."

"Well, maybe," she said, laughing. As she moved to the side of the mare, she lifted the reins over the horse's head and reached for the saddle horn.

"Do you need some help getting on?"

Her laugh was shaky. "You don't have a lot of faith in me, do you?"

"I didn't mean—"

"I know you didn't," she said, looking back at him.

"What you *can* do is let me give it a try. If I can't do it, I'll bow to your expertise and ask for your help."

He considered it, and finally stepped back. "Okay," he relented. But if her foot slipped or anything else happened, he'd be ready.

Her first attempt to boost herself up in the stirrup and swing the other leg over the saddle failed, but he gritted his teeth and didn't rush forward to help. For that, she graced him with an appreciative smile.

"You'll get it this time," he told her.

"I will." Her shoulders rose and fell with a deep breath, and then she swung her right leg over, settling gracefully into the saddle. "I did it!"

The first thing he noticed, after admiring how great she looked on the horse, was that he'd guessed wrong at the length of the stirrups. It was going to be practically impossible to fix them without getting close to her. But he didn't have a choice.

"Those stirrups need adjusting," he said, without looking at her. "I'll fix them."

He felt her lean down to watch him. As he changed the length, he heard her say, "My legs are a little longer than you thought."

He looked up at her, and their gazes caught. He could only imagine what those long legs could do. Suddenly realizing where his thoughts were going, he looked down and forced himself to concentrate on what he was doing. "A little."

It didn't take him long to adjust both stirrups. "Perfect," she announced when he was done, and urged her horse forward. "So where are we riding?"

He quickly mounted his own horse. "I was thinking we could ride down to Lake Walker."

She looked back over her shoulder at him. "Lake Walker? I don't think I'm familiar with that."

"Erin named it," he explained, catching up with her. "Most people would call it a farm pond, but it's a lot bigger than that. When we were old enough to get away with it, we put a trolling motor on a rowboat and took it out on the water. Sometimes we'd spend a whole day out there just fishing."

"Did you catch anything?"

Suddenly hit with a clear memory of those times, he hesitated before answering. "Sometimes. When Pop would remember to stock it."

"What about the rowboat? Is it still there?"

He'd pulled it out of the water the summer after the accident, stowed the motor in the barn and never thought about it again. Until now.

"I don't know," he answered, not wanting to admit what he'd done. "I haven't been down there for a long time."

"Could we look for it? Would you mind? Maybe it's still there and seaworthy." A sheepish grin replaced her excitement. "Or pondworthy, at least."

"Sure, we can look." He didn't want her to get her hopes up. Fifteen years had probably taken a toll on the wooden boat. "But don't be disappointed if we don't find it or it's in bad shape."

They rode out of the yard and started across the wide pasture at a leisurely pace. "I'd forgotten how beautiful the wildflowers are," she said when they'd ridden for several minutes. "I never had a chance to see them when I was living in Texas with my mom."

Something in her voice caused him to look over at her, but her expression didn't give away anything. "What did you do in Texas?"

"I got an education. I'd never had the opportunity before."

"You went to college there?"

"Yes." She turned her head to look at him, her smile lighting her face. "And I have the diploma to prove it."

"Good for you."

There were times when he wished he could say the same, but he'd made the choice to turn down a college scholarship and focus instead on the ranch. Both would have made his parents proud, had they been there, but they weren't and he'd needed to make amends.

With his thoughts still on the past, it took him a second to realize he could see Lake Walker up ahead. He'd forgotten how peaceful it had always made him feel. It hadn't changed much, except that the trees around it had grown to reach higher in the sky.

"Dylan?"

"Yeah?" he answered, his attention still on the view ahead.

"That's it, right? The pond, I mean."

"Yeah, that's it." Seeing it nearly took his breath away, and he was suddenly glad that he hadn't visited again until now.

When he turned to see her reaction, she was looking at him. "No wonder Erin named it *Lake* Walker," she said. "It's huge."

At the sound of a splash, Dylan gazed out at the water. "Must be a fish in there."

"Look," she said, pointing out to the middle of the pond. "I can see the ripples. It has to be a fish. Or several fish." She looked back at him. "Wouldn't that be something?"

He vaguely remembered that his dad had restocked the pond early that last spring, long before the weather turned warm and storms had begun rumbling. Those fish must have kept the pond populated.

"Luke is going to love this," he said.

"He likes to fish?"

"He loves it. More than I do."

"Did your dad fish?"

Bits and pieces that he hadn't thought of for years started coming back to him. "No, not much. He spent most of his time working, keeping the ranch going." He turned back to look behind them. "He and Mom used to watch us from the house. Or at least that's what they said. I suppose they could see us from one of the upstairs windows."

"What wonderful memories you must have."

As he turned back, all he could do was nod. He wasn't sure he wanted those memories to resurface. They were often painful when they did.

"What about the boat?" she asked. "Where do you think it might be?"

He surveyed the area, trying to remember where he'd pulled it ashore. Getting his bearings in an area changed by fifteen years of growth, he pointed to his left. "Over there, maybe."

"Let's go look." Swinging her leg over Cinnamon's side, she dismounted.

Nodding, he did the same. "I don't think the horses will wander off, but just in case, let's tie them to that tree over there. Give me your reins."

When she handed them to him, her fingers brushed his, and he felt electricity shoot through him. Unable to stop himself, he looked at her, and it was clear that she must have felt it, too. He instinctively pulled back, knowing that if he didn't, he might lose control and do something they both might regret.

While he concentrated on tying the reins to the tree, he sensed her moving away. Giving a final tug to make sure the reins were secure, he looked up to find her gone. "Glory?" he called.

"Over here."

Walking toward the sound of her voice, he suspected she'd found the boat and, considering the disappointment he heard, he guessed it was in bad condition. He almost wished it wasn't, but from experience, he knew wishing was a waste of time.

"OH, GOOD GRIEF." GLORY MUTTERED a few unladylike words under her breath while she pulled on the thick strand of hair that had caught in a bramble bush. It was bad enough that she'd found the boat, only to discover the rotted boards in the bottom of it, and now this.

"Looks like you've got a problem."

Squeezing her eyes shut, she took a deep breath, and then opened them to see him standing nearby. Up until now, it had been such a great day, and here she'd gone and managed to get herself tangled up in a bush. "I don't know how I managed to do this."

"I should have warned you. Erin always said these bushes had a thing for hair. Luke and I never had that problem."

Unable to move and embarrassed for foolishly not watching where she was going, she waited patiently as he walked toward her. "One more reason to get a buzz cut," she said, laughing.

"You'd start a new fad, for sure."

"Ha. As if anyone cares what I— Ouch!"

"Damn," he whispered. "Sorry. Just let me…"

She couldn't turn her head to see his face and hoped

he couldn't see hers. "Maybe now would be a good time for that buzz cut."

"I can get it. I never had to cut Erin's hair, and believe me, she never paid any attention to where she was going."

"I've always admired her. She was such a tomboy and seemed to have so much fun."

He grunted at the description of his sister. "Tomboy? Well, that's one way of putting it. Mama used to say she was a hoyden, but until I was older, I didn't know what that meant."

"She has a good heart," Glory said. If it hadn't been for his sister buying her saddle, she wouldn't have had the money to pay off the back taxes on her grandmother's building and start her business. But that was something he didn't need to know.

"Yeah, she does," he answered.

"And so do you." The words were out of her mouth before she could stop them. She wished she'd kept quiet.

"Glory—"

Her heart gave a little skip when he said her name. "What?"

There was a pause before he answered. "I think I've got it. Yeah, your hair's loose."

Relief, tinged with a bit of disappointment, washed through her. "Really?"

"Yeah. Come on, I'll help you up."

Before she had a chance to answer, she saw his hand reaching down to her. For a split second, she wondered if it was safe to take it, considering her recent reactions to even the simple touch from him. She was being silly, she told herself. She put her hand in his, only to become breathless at the strength she felt in it. He pulled her to her feet, and before she knew what was happening, she was upright.

"Thanks," she murmured. He was so close, she could feel his warmth. Looking up, she discovered him watching her. "You were right, you know."

"About what?" he asked, his voice rough as his gaze seemed to see right into her.

"The b-boat," she stammered and pointed to the row-boat. "It's broken."

For a second, he was silent and still. "Yeah, it is."

Frozen in the moment, she waited, holding her breath and wishing he'd kiss her again. She knew it would be wrong. No matter what she felt for him, she had to deny it. Understanding that in the past, she'd been eager to please others when she shouldn't have, she'd sworn off relationships. But even knowing all that, when he moved to touch her cheek, she closed her eyes, memorizing every tiny detail of how it felt. This was what she had missed. No one had ever been this gentle with her, but she'd imagined. She'd dreamed.

She felt the whisper of a breath on her skin before she felt his lips capture hers. Her knees weakened, and she leaned into him, only to feel him gather her into his arms, pulling her even closer. As he slowly deepened the kiss, she wondered if she'd died and gone to heaven.

Wishes do come true. Even when they shouldn't.

Chapter Nine

Sitting on the blanket he'd spread on the ground, Dylan skimmed a rock on the surface of the pond. He knew he shouldn't have kissed Glory, but he hadn't been able to stop himself. That had to change. They could be friends, but they couldn't be— He blocked the word from his mind. They couldn't be anything more. Even friends was a risk, but he'd take it.

None of that meant he was going to let this chance to spend some time with her slip through his fingers. He'd just have to remember to keep some space between them.

Beside him, but not too close, Glory tossed her own rock, and it sank. She let out a loud sigh, and then laughed. "I guess I wasn't cut out for rock skimming."

"You need more practice, that's all."

"As if there's time for that." A silence fell between them, until she spoke again. "You've done wonders with this ranch."

He tossed another rock. "Thanks, but it wasn't just me. Luke has always played a big part in the ranch. I couldn't have done it alone."

His sister had played a big part, too. She'd kept them afloat for the first few years. She'd kept him sane. If it hadn't been for her, he might have done something they all would have regretted. He owed Erin, just as much as he owed Luke.

"I envy you your family," she said. "I always wished for a sister or a brother. My friends had siblings, and I'd see them fight, and I'd wish I had that."

"We fought a lot, Luke and Erin and me. Still do, sometimes. But I guess that's just part of it."

She traced the plaid pattern on the blanket with a finger and nodded. "It probably kept you all together. Fighting involves emotions. You wouldn't have fought if you hadn't cared."

He turned to study her. The more he'd been around her, the more he learned. Her eyes revealed a lot, but not always enough to understand. She'd been the Golden Girl, always happy, always smiling and laughing. But at that moment, her smile was gone, and he felt there was a lot more to Glory than he and maybe everyone else suspected.

"How was North Carolina?" he asked, hoping to learn more about what had brought her back to Desperation and into his life.

She raised her head to stare out toward the water. "Charlotte is beautiful and the people are wonderful."

"That kind of sounds rehearsed," he said, without thinking. But it was true.

"In a sense, I guess it is." She turned her head to look at him. "You want to know why Kyle and I are divorced."

It wasn't a question, but a statement, and all he could do was nod. "Sure, I'm curious. My guess is that everybody is, at least a little."

Her smile didn't reach her eyes. "I'd be surprised if they weren't, but it wouldn't do any good to tell them. Nobody would believe me."

His curiosity leaped from simple to burning. "Try me."

There was a flash of pain in her eyes before she turned away. "It wasn't just Charlotte," she said. "It started a long time before that."

He didn't doubt it. "You and Kyle were a couple—"

"Because that's what we were supposed to be."

He continued to watch her as she stared at the water again. She didn't seem to be very willing to explain, but he couldn't let it go. "What do you mean?"

Shaking her head, she sighed. "That's the way he wanted it."

"He? You mean Kyle?"

"No, not Kyle. My father."

He wasn't sure he heard her right. "Your *father?*"

"Forget it."

When she started to move away, he reached for her, but stopped short of actually touching her. "Wait. Don't go. You don't have to tell me anything."

She looked at him, her beautiful face marred by pain. With a slight nod, she settled on the blanket again.

He didn't want to push her. He had his own secrets. He understood the need to keep them. But not being much of a conversationalist, he wasn't sure what else he could say to fill the silence that now existed between them.

"I'm here to listen. Or not," he said, hoping it would help. When she didn't respond, he was convinced he'd ruined the day and was about to suggest they mount up and head home.

"I know everybody thinks I've led a charmed life, but I haven't," she said, surprising him.

He had a problem believing it. She'd always had a smile on her face and a kind word for everyone. She hadn't been one of those stuck-up girls. Even his sister had had nice things to say about Glory when they were in school, and Erin didn't always get along with everyone.

She turned to look at him, a strange mixture of sadness and a hard, stubborn glitter in her eyes. "You're one of them. You think it was all sunshine, with parades and crowns and roses. Well, you're wrong."

He knew he needed to say something to keep her talking, so he did. "Okay."

"Nobody knows the truth."

"They never do."

She stared at her hands, folded in her lap. "Gram knows some of it, but not all. Even Kyle doesn't know a lot of it. But then he wouldn't have cared if he had."

That surprised Dylan, but he didn't say so. She'd already gotten upset once. If he said the wrong thing again, she might never tell him anything. He had a feeling she needed someone to talk to—someone she could trust—and he was determined to be that someone. At least he could do that much.

"It was my dad's idea that Kyle and I should get together," she said. "That was after he'd decided that I needed to try out for cheerleading. Grades weren't all that important to him, just the fact that people liked me and paid attention to me." She turned to him again. "That way he got attention, too."

Dylan had known Glen Caldwell, although not well. He hadn't paid a lot of attention to the parents of the people he'd gone to school with, unless they were friends of his mom or dad. Mr. Caldwell had never struck him as a friend of anyone's. He didn't recall his parents ever saying anything about the man, except one time when his dad had called the guy a wheeler-dealer. It hadn't been said in an especially nice way. Still, that didn't mean a whole lot.

But Dylan was confused by what she'd said. "You didn't want to be a cheerleader?"

She shrugged. "Not really. All I wanted to do was draw. When I was very young, I remember my mother dressing me in pretty things and telling me how happy I would make Daddy. It wasn't until I was older that I realized I was really little more than a tool for him. And if I didn't meet his standards…" She turned away with a shrug.

An icy chill went through him. "He hurt you?"

She didn't even glance at him when she said, "Not so much after I realized that all I had to do was be popular."

He couldn't wrap his mind around any man doing that to a child. "Didn't your mother—"

"She didn't know about the bruises on my arms from being dragged to my room and locked inside. After the one time he hit me with his belt, I gave in and became the daughter he wanted."

Looking down, he saw that she had clenched her hands into fists, her knuckles white. If he'd had any thoughts that she wasn't being completely truthful, he didn't anymore.

"Kyle didn't know about this?" he asked, thinking the man she married must have had a clue.

"Only that I did what I was told." Her shoulders slumped with resignation, but she looked at him. "If he knew, he never said anything. He was always too wrapped up in himself."

Dylan had heard that a battered child was more likely to marry another batterer. "Did Kyle hit you, too?"

She shook her head. "No. He never hit me. He never

did anything like that to me. I was his trophy wife. He wouldn't have put a mark on me. Besides, that would have taken more energy than he would ever expend on me. I was there to make him respectable, so no one would know about the other women."

Anger shot through him. "He cheated on you?"

"That's what happens when two young people marry because their parents think it's the right thing to do."

Dylan knew that most everyone in Desperation had thought Glory and Kyle were living a fairy-tale life in North Carolina. He'd been in the café several times when Kyle's grandmother had passed around pictures of their fancy house for everyone to see. He'd never liked Letha Atkins or her grandson, but he wasn't raised to say so, and he wouldn't now.

"I didn't know," he said instead.

"And you shouldn't now." She put her hand on his. "I guess I just needed to unload. You're a very special man, Dylan. I hope you know that."

He might have been okay if she hadn't moved closer and kissed his cheek. When she did that, he couldn't keep himself from reaching for her. Before he knew what he'd done, he'd leaned back on the blanket and pulled her on top of him, while he kissed her the way he'd been wanting to for weeks. He didn't know how to stop his growing feelings for her. While he knew it could never work out for them, there was a part of him that didn't want to let her go.

GLORY BLOCKED OUT the warnings in her head, telling her she was moving into dangerous territory. It was completely wrong for her to get involved with Dylan in any other way besides professionally. But she couldn't deny that having his arms around her made her feel more wanted than she ever remembered. His kisses burned right through her, and she secretly wished they would never stop.

Reaching for the top button of his shirt, she easily undid it. Ready to move on to the next and all the others, she didn't expect to find herself on her back beneath him, while he trailed kisses along her jaw. She finished with the buttons, and her hands explored him as she memorized every muscle and curve.

He moved away just enough so that she could see his face. His eyes were dark with a passion that took her by surprise. She'd never experienced anything like what was happening to her at that moment, but she was ready for it. More than ready.

As if their minds and bodies were in perfect sync, he moved to kick off his boots, while she reached for the bottom of her knit top. Before she could pull it up, he brushed her hands aside and slowly peeled it up and over her head. In what seemed like seconds, they were both lying naked on the blanket, exploring each other with their hands and mouths.

When he slowly entered her, she was more than ready. She welcomed him with a desire she'd never imagined was possible. For a brief moment, she understood what had been missing in her life, and then the thought was gone, swept away by feeling and touching and tasting.

He guided her to sensations she'd never known, and when it was his turn, she could barely breathe.

They didn't speak or even move to uncouple when their breathing slowed to near normal. "Glory," he said, his voice rough.

She pressed her palm to his cheek. "Not now."

But instead of seeing the smile she'd been wishing

for, he eased away, taking his warmth with him. "Maybe we should be heading back," he said, his face showing no emotion.

Without a word, they sorted through the clothing that lay scattered around them. When they'd finished dressing in silence, he got to his feet and held out his hand to help her up.

She suspected she'd disappointed him, but she couldn't dwell on that. Right now, she had to focus on other things or she'd never make it through this.

It wasn't far to the spot where the horses were tethered, and within minutes they were mounted again and on their way back to the barn. She sneaked a quick look at him before they approached the ancient but sturdy barn, and couldn't help but notice how tight his strong jaw appeared. Was he wishing he'd never invited her to ride? Was he wishing she'd go away and not come back?

"I'll take care of the horses," he said as they dismounted and he took her horse's reins.

Glory winced. "I don't mind helping with—"

"No, it's right that I do. I invited you to ride."

And he was wishing he hadn't—she was certain of that. "Thank you," she managed to say, following him into the barn. Unsure of what to say or do next, she decided that leaving would be her best choice. "I guess I'll see you tomorrow."

He put each of the horses into a stall, and then turned to her. "No, not tomorrow."

She wanted to ask where he was going, but she couldn't. She sensed it would be wrong, in spite of what had taken place between them at the pond. She nodded, not knowing what she should say.

"It was a mistake."

For a moment, she didn't understand, and stood staring at him, unable to speak. "I don't—" But she couldn't finish. Shadows danced across his face in the low light of the barn as he stood there, his gaze averted.

White-hot pain shot through her. "I'll finish up the work while you're gone and then I'll—" What? There was nothing else. There never had been. She turned away and walked through the big door and out into the sunshine.

THE NEXT MORNING at breakfast, Glory vowed to put the day before out of her mind. She had a job to finish at Dylan's house, and she desperately needed to get past what had happened to do it.

"Did you enjoy your ride?" her grandmother asked.

Sitting at the kitchen table, Glory managed a smile. She should have known it wouldn't be that easy. "It was very nice."

Not only was she dealing with Dylan's parting words, but she was still grappling with the enormity of revealing so much of her life to someone who now ranked their lovemaking as a mistake. She shouldn't have told him about her father or even Kyle. But at least she'd been given a reprieve for a couple of days and a chance to sort through everything—especially the revelation that she'd been totally wrong about him.

"You look tired, Glory. Maybe you should take a break. I don't think Dylan would mind, would he?"

Glory set her fork down on her plate. "Whether he does or not, he probably wouldn't say so. I'm never quite sure what he's thinking." But that wasn't true. She'd known exactly what he was thinking the day before. *It was a mistake.*

"Still waters run deep," Louise announced, her attention on the toast she was buttering.

"So I've heard." Glory focused on her own plate, afraid her grandmother might be able to guess something had happened. She wasn't sure if she should be more concerned that she hadn't felt any need for restraint with someone who obviously didn't feel anywhere near the same about her as she did about him, or that she'd shared things with him that she'd only shared with the counselor she'd seen in Texas at her mother's insistence. Both were tearing her apart.

Feeling antsy, she pushed her chair back and stood. "I'd better get busy."

"What's on your schedule today?"

Glory grabbed her bag from the chair near the door. "Odds and ends, mostly. I shouldn't be late, but I'll call if I will be," she said over her shoulder as she opened the door and stepped out onto the sidewalk.

Fifteen minutes later, she turned her car into the lane at the ranch and pulled to a stop in front of the house. Shutting off the engine, she looked around to see if anyone was there, but even Erin's motor home was gone from the place where it had been parked, although the horse trailer was still there. Glory slipped her bag over her shoulder, climbed out of the car and shut the door. At least it would be quiet, although she expected her three helpers to arrive soon.

Stepping into the unlocked house, she decided to start with a thorough walk-through to see if she'd missed anything that might need some attention. Flashlight in one hand, small voice recorder in the other, she began in the kitchen.

While inspecting each of the rooms, she was filled with pride at the work she'd done. She hoped it might lead to more decorating jobs and that if Erin planned a long visit, she might help with a little word-of-mouth advertising.

Making a final voice note in the upstairs cloud room, her voice cracked. She ignored it and the rush of feelings that made her heart ache.

There were still things left to be done to the room, so she put her stuff down and got to work. After pouring paint into the roller pan, she went into the closet where she'd found the box of journals.

Mindless work, she told herself as the paint rolled onto the closet wall, brightening the off-white paint that had yellowed with age. It was good for the soul, her grandfather used to tell her. As she reached toward the ceiling, she missed him even more than she had twelve years before, when he'd died.

Stepping out of the closet, she pulled the small step-ladder inside it with her, determined to put the sadness of the past and the present aside. "The future will be brighter," she whispered and concentrated on painting as much of the ceiling as she could reach, without dripping paint on the wood floor.

"It's time to grow up," she continued in the silence of the old house. "Time to be strong." She squeezed her eyes shut. "And just how does one do—"

The paint roller hit a bump, and a fairly solid one, she guessed. Switching the roller to her left hand, she stretched as far as she could and, with her right hand, tentatively touched the spot that had grabbed her attention. Sure enough, there was something there that she hadn't noticed before.

Ignoring the sticky paint, she managed to follow a wide ridge with her fingers and realized she'd just discovered a covered opening to what she guessed was the attic. Why hadn't she thought about checking for one?

She'd stepped down from the short ladder when she heard a voice in the hallway. "Miz Andrews, are you up here?"

"In here," she answered. Placing the roller in the paint tray, she left the closet.

Seconds later, Stu walked into the room. "Mark had to run a quick errand, but he'll be here in a few minutes. Is there something I can do to help?"

She nodded. "You certainly can. I found an opening to what I'm sure is the attic," she said, pointing into the closet. "I'll need a ladder that will reach into it, once I can open the panel keeping it closed."

"Yeah, sure," he said. "I'm pretty sure I saw one in the equipment shed. If the building isn't locked, I can get it."

"It'll reach up into the opening in there?"

He ducked into the closet and quickly reappeared. "Shouldn't be a problem."

"Great!" While he left to get the ladder, she continued to paint, hoping it might help temper her excitement. There was no telling what she might find in the attic, if anything. Besides, it kept her from thinking about other things.

It seemed like an eternity passed before both Stu and Mark returned with the ladder. In no time at all, they had the attic open and the ladder placed so she could climb up and through the opening.

"Would you hand me my flashlight?" she asked. Tucking it under one arm, she took each rung carefully.

Before she reached the top of the ladder, she was halfway into the attic. Shining the light around the large, dusty space, she was disappointed that there wasn't more there. An old lamp that had seen better days had been put in a corner, and a broken rocking chair sat near a small air vent. But it was the box she spied within her reach that claimed her attention and caused her heart to beat a little quicker. Hoping it might contain a small treasure of some kind, she pulled it toward her.

"I've found something," she said, "but I'm not sure I can get it down."

"We'll get it for you," Mark and Stu said in unison.

She climbed down the ladder, eager to see what she'd unearthed. When Stu finally handed her the large box Mark had retrieved, she immediately placed it on the floor and sat next to it.

"Thank you," she told them, wanting to open the box alone. "Take the rest of the day off."

"But—"

"I'll make a list tonight of what last-minute things need to be done tomorrow."

Once the boys were gone, she carefully pulled the lid off the box and looked inside. She wasn't disappointed. The box was filled with pictures of the Walker family, and she knew exactly what she would do with them.

DYLAN ORDERED ANOTHER round for the group of friends gathered at Lou's to see Erin before she left town again. As he watched, he realized how much he'd missed his sister. He and Luke and Erin had been as thick as thieves when they were kids, but after the accident—and especially after Erin left when Luke turned eighteen—things changed. If it hadn't been for the fact that he and Luke had taken on the ranch, he had a feeling they all would have gone their separate ways. Erin sure had.

"So you're going back to ride the circuit," Dusty said to her from across the table.

"It's what I do best," she answered, pushing the untouched beer glass away with one finger. "I see *you've* done all right for yourself, since retiring. I could hardly believe it when I heard you'd married Kate, but it's pretty easy to see that it was supposed to be."

Dusty grinned and pushed his cowboy hat farther back on his head with a finger. "She sure beats gettin' banged up riding bulls."

When Kate punched her husband's arm, Dylan felt a quick stab of envy. If only he could've had something like Dusty had. But fearing losing someone else he loved, he'd chosen a different path and learned to live with his solitude. Or thought he had, until Glory walked into his house and everything changed. He just didn't know what to do about it. Even worse, he suspected he'd probably destroyed any chance he might have had with her, considering what he'd said to her when they left the pond.

Erin, in the seat next to him, looked around at everyone sitting at the tables they'd shoved together. "Y'all make me feel young again."

Luke, on the other side of her, snorted in the midst of the laughter. "Yeah, like you're some old lady."

"I'm older than you," she pointed out. "All of you."

"Hey!"

Everyone turned to look at Tanner O'Brien, sitting with his wife, Jules. "I can remember when I was in high school and you were in grade school, little miss." That brought more laughter. "I have five years on you, so let's not talk about old, you hear?"

Erin's face turned bright red as she laughed with the others. "I'll keep that in mind, especially since you have one of those fancy NRCA Championship buckles."

There was more talk and reminiscing between the dozen or so people who'd come to see an old friend whom many had known since childhood. Dylan wished some things had been different for his sister and brother, but they both seemed happy.

The evening grew later, and one by one the friends began to leave. The stragglers still sat at one end of the table, obviously trying to make the night last a little longer. Luke sat talking to Tanner about the O'Briens' and McPhersons' latest sales of some of their rodeo stock, while Erin sat nearby, talking with their wives. When Dylan felt a hand on his shoulder, he looked up to see Tanner's brother.

"Hey, Dylan, there's a baseball game planned for the Fourth of July celebration this year," Tucker said, pulling up a chair next to him and straddling it. "Shawn's home from college for the summer, and he wanted me to ask if you might be interested in playing on his team."

Dylan shook his head. "I haven't played since—" He still didn't find it easy to talk about, but he continued. "Not since high school. I'm not sure I even remember how to catch a ball, much less throw one."

Dusty joined them and sat on the other side of Tucker. "If I can give it a try, you can, too."

"You were never a ballplayer, Dusty. All you ever wanted to do was ride bulls. Are you sure you want to give it a try now?"

Dusty shrugged and leaned back. "I might as well. It couldn't be any more dangerous than those bulls were. You need to join us, Dylan. We might not win, but we'll have a damn good time playing."

But playing baseball was something Dylan had sworn never to do again after his parents died, and he was relieved when the others began to head toward the exit. Turning to Tucker, he said, "Tell Shawn thanks for thinking of me, but not this time."

"Seems to me you said something similar about the box social," Dusty said, leaning forward. "That turned out pretty good, didn't it?"

Too good, Dylan thought, but he'd made his decision to spend his life as a bachelor. It was safer. And baseball was out of the question.

"I guess you could say the box social turned out okay," he said, answering Dusty's question. "Glory and I are friends." That sounded kind of lame, so he added, "And if your wives ever want some decorating done, you make sure they get in touch with her. She knows what she's doing."

"Yeah, we'll do that," Tucker said, glancing at Dusty.

Dylan felt someone behind him put a hand on his shoulder, and looked back to see his brother.

"The party's breaking up," Luke said. "Erin's ready to leave. I'll meet you both outside."

Dylan nodded and got to his feet. After telling his friends goodbye, he looked for his sister, and the two of them left the tavern together.

"Did I hear Tucker and Dusty ask if you'd play on some baseball team?" she asked as they headed for Luke's truck.

Dylan didn't want to talk about it, but if he didn't answer, Erin would badger him all the way home. "Something like that, yeah."

"You're going to do it, aren't you?"

Instead of being truthful about it, he answered with, "I'll think about it."

"I certainly hope so," she announced in her big-sister voice. "Don't let me find out you didn't."

"Right." But he had no intention of becoming involved in anything resembling baseball.

Luke joined them as they reached the pickup and

they all climbed inside. They were on the road that would take them back to the ranch when Erin, sitting between them, let out a long sigh.

"What?" Luke asked, glancing at her.

Looking like the cat that had swallowed the canary, she smiled sweetly at Dylan, and then at Luke. "I've done a pretty good job, don't you think?"

Luke looked over the top of her head at Dylan before answering her. "What do you mean?"

"Why, look at you, Luke Walker," she said. "You found the right woman for you and the perfect mama for your son."

In the darkness of the pickup cab, Dylan heard his brother grunt. "I knew you were playing matchmaker, big sister, and you're just lucky it worked out, that's all."

"You think so?" Still smiling, she turned to Dylan. "I didn't do so bad for you, either, did I?"

Dylan looked at her through narrowed eyes as his blood chilled in his veins. "What are you talking about?"

"I'm talking about Glory. Admit it. You have a thing for her, and I know she has one for you." Her chuckle was soft and tinged with wickedness as she glanced from one brother to the other. "You two really should thank me for the women in your lives."

Over the top of her head, Dylan caught Luke's attention. No words passed between them, until they arrived at the ranch, and Erin told them both good-night before disappearing in the dark as she walked on to her motor home.

"She set us both up," Luke said.

Dylan shook his head, his anger at her making him want to punch something. "She's going to regret this. I'm going to make sure of it."

"Yeah," Luke said. "She needs to be taught a lesson about meddling in other people's business."

"Agreed."

"But how?"

Dylan shook his head. "I don't know, but we'll find a way."

"The sooner the better."

"Damn straight."

Chapter Ten

"Are you sure you'll be delivering it today?" Glory asked the man on the phone.

"Yes, ma'am. In fact, I saw to it myself that it was loaded on the truck."

She wasn't convinced. She needed that delivery today so she could finish the gift she'd started for Dylan. After the incident at the pond, she'd been sorely tempted to forget about it and cancel the project, but she couldn't. In the grand scheme of things, what had happened that day didn't matter.

Now the question had become if her order would arrive on time. Fifty miles from the city could mean being at the end of the list, but the man seemed sure there wouldn't be a problem. "All right. I'll hold you to that."

After saying goodbye, she ended the call just in time to make the turn onto the ranch property. To her immense relief, she didn't see any sign of Dylan and hadn't seen him since they'd ridden to the pond, five days before. For that she was thankful.

Instead of getting out of the car, she stared at the house in front of her and thought about how well she'd been able to keep things she didn't want to think about locked away. She'd learned at an early age, thanks to her father, and had honed the gift to perfection during her marriage. It had served her well, and the only time the lock hadn't held was one night when she was on the phone with her mom.

Learning that Kyle had a mistress had been bad enough, but discovering that his infidelity had been going on since early in their marriage, she'd been devastated. She'd never meant to bare her tattered soul to her mother, but, just as it had with Dylan, the truth had all come spilling out when her mother called from Texas one night to say hello. A week later, a check for a thousand dollars arrived from her mother, with a note inviting her to live in Texas whenever she decided to leave. Another week later, Glory had shipped her things to her mother and was on a plane to Dallas.

The only thing Glory regretted was not doing it sooner. Although she and her mother had never been very close when she was a child, that changed, too. Together, they found common ground, happy to finally be not only a real mother and daughter, but friends.

If only she could lock away the memories of the horseback ride she'd shared with Dylan. She didn't want to, but he'd made it clear that he didn't feel the same as she did and was now wishing it hadn't happened. But she finally had faith in herself that she would not only survive, but handle it without letting it get in the way of her dream.

Pulled from her reverie by the sound of a vehicle, she turned to see whom it might be and recognized Luke's fiancée driving the car that pulled up and stopped beside her. Getting out of her own car, she waved to Hayley before removing a box from the backseat.

"Looks like you came prepared," Hayley said, walking up to Glory's car.

"I try." Smiling, Glory nodded toward another box. "There's a smaller one. Would you mind bringing it in?"

"Not at all." Hayley grabbed the box and followed Glory into the house. "Wherever did you find all of these?"

Glory shrugged as she carried her box into the dining room and set it on the table. "Here and there," she answered. While Hayley placed her box next to the other, Glory pulled out one of the fifty-some frames she'd found. "A lot of them were in the upstairs of the shop. Apparently my great-grandmother—my grandfather's mother—had a thing for frames. Not only did she put photos in them, but pretty things that pleased her and anything else that struck her fancy. Gram had never had the heart to get rid of them."

"They're beautiful," Hayley said, taking two out of the box. "So different than the ones we can buy now."

"Which is why I thought they'd be perfect for the photos I found. I'm so glad you decided to come today."

Hayley pulled out a few more picture frames. "Monday is my day off, so when Luke asked if I might be free to help, I was happy to say I could. Where did you say you found the photos?"

Glory felt her face warm. "I probably shouldn't tell you, since I didn't have permission to go snooping—which I wasn't," she quickly added, "but I discovered an opening to the attic while painting in a closet."

"I can imagine how excited you were. Luke said he'd try to stop by later to take a look at them, but he and Dylan have a pretty full day."

Realizing that she wouldn't be encountering Dylan until later, Glory relaxed and nodded. "If you'll take the frames out and sort them by sizes, I'll get the photos from the pantry."

She was almost through the kitchen on her way to the pantry, where she'd left the box of pictures, when she heard the porch door open. Knowing without having to look that it was Dylan, she stopped in the doorway near his office. In spite of what had happened between them, she wanted to surprise him with the pictures, so she had to be careful that he didn't suspect anything.

"Good morning," she said, trying for a smile when he walked into the kitchen.

He stopped just inside the door. "I saw your car outside."

Nodding, she swallowed the nervous lump in her throat. "I'm doing some last-minute touch-ups. I did a walk-through last week and found some things that needed some work."

A frown drew his mouth down. "Anything major?"

"No, no," she hurried to say. "Just little things. Hayley is here lending a hand, so it shouldn't take long. I'm guessing we'll be done later this afternoon and—"

"No hurry," he said before she finished. "I just came in for…" He glanced around the room. "I need to get some papers in my office."

She realized she was blocking the doorway. "Sorry. I'll get out of your way and see you later, then."

He'd stepped past her and into the hallway, but stopped to look back. "Yeah, later."

When he disappeared, Glory blew out a breath. She felt as though she was fifteen again. And had sounded like it, too, she thought, swallowing a groan.

With Dylan in his office, she quickly and quietly removed the box of pictures from the pantry and joined Hayley again in the dining room. Pleased at the ease of her escape, she began sorting photos.

"Don't run away from it, Glory."

Glory's hand stilled on the frame she was about to pick up. Instinct told her exactly what Hayley was referring to, but she decided to play dumb. Looking at Hayley, standing next to her, she said, "I'm sorry. What?"

"It wasn't that long ago that I was in the same place."

"I don't—"

"Yes, you do. You know exactly what I'm talking about. I spent weeks denying it, too."

Glancing out the door toward the hallway where Dylan might appear at any moment, she worried he might overhear their conversation. "I don't mean to be unkind," she said, keeping her voice low, just in case, "but I really don't want to talk about whatever it is you're thinking."

With an understanding smile, Hayley walked to the door and shut it. "One problem solved." Returning to where Glory stood, she took her by the hand and led her out of the room, through the living room and then outside to the porch. "Second problem solved. Now let's move on to the big one."

Still not convinced she wanted to talk about how she felt, she shook her head. "I don't have a problem."

Hayley's smile was accompanied by a sigh. Settling on one of the steps, she motioned for Glory to join her, and then waited until she did before speaking. "That's what we always say. I can admit now that I had a problem with trust and was unwilling to allow anyone in my life who I thought might take over. I was lucky and found the right man, in spite of it."

Glory couldn't argue with that. "Yes, you were. But it isn't easy and I'm getting too old to make a mistake like the last one."

"Old? You?" Hayley patted her arm. "Then I must be getting up there in years, too."

Even Glory realized how ridiculous she'd sounded and laughed. "You're right."

"And I'm right that you shouldn't run from this. Dylan has his ghosts from the past, but then we all do. It could be that what he needs is a good woman to help him put them to rest."

"I'll keep that in mind," Glory said. But she wasn't sure if it mattered. She didn't know how Dylan felt about her, and she had enough disappointments in her life, not to mention a business to grow.

Relieved when she heard Dylan's truck start and saw him drive away, she stood. "Let's go see if we can find some frames for some pictures."

But even after they began matching photos to frames, Glory couldn't forget what Hayley had said. The big question was whether Dylan was at all interested. At times she believed he was, and at others, it was as if he wished she would vanish. But other than asking him straight-out, she wasn't sure how she would ever know.

DYLAN WINCED AT the sound of the little bell that announced his entrance into the shop. A quick glance told him he was alone.

"I'll be with you in a minute," a woman called from a distance.

"No hurry," he said, and pulled off his cowboy hat as Louise Gardner appeared from around a corner.

"Oh! Hello there, Dylan. Glory isn't here—"

"Yeah, I know," he said. "She's still working at the house. Last-minute stuff, she said."

"All right," she said slowly.

Nervous, he cleared his throat. "I have something for her."

"Oh, how nice. But wouldn't it be better if you gave it to her in person?"

He shook his head. He wasn't doing a very good job of this. "I want it to be a surprise. You see, I have the saddle that her grandfather—I mean, your husband—made for her."

"*You* have it? How did it—"

"My sister bought it from her down in Texas. I bought it from my sister." *After* he'd talked her into finally selling it to him. "Is there somewhere I can put it? The workshop, maybe?"

She looked behind her, toward the back of the shop, before answering. "Oh, I don't know. Nobody has been out there to straighten and clean for, oh, I can't remember."

Glancing at his watch, he calculated how much time he might have. This was too important to him to give up easily. "Maybe I can clean it up a little and make some space."

She shook her head. "I couldn't ask you to do that."

"You aren't asking, ma'am. I'm offering."

He wasn't sure what he saw as she studied his face, but she finally nodded. "Yes, maybe a little. Glory would like that, even without the saddle."

Now he was getting somewhere. "I don't have a lot of time," he cautioned.

She motioned for him to follow her. "Anything would be better than it is now. Neither Glory nor I— Let's just say it's not easy for us to be in the place where Abe spent so much of his time."

"Understandable."

Opening the door that led directly into the workshop, she pointed to the far corner. "There's a saddle stand over there. Do you have the saddle with you?"

"It's in the back of my truck."

When she smiled, her eyes twinkled. "Perfect. When there's space for the stand, unlock that big door, and you can pull your truck around back."

He thanked her and added, "I can't stay long, but I'll do as much as I can."

She pressed her hand to his arm. "It's not your mess, Dylan. It's ours."

"I'm happy to do whatever I can."

She smiled again. "And I'm glad for that. Now I'll leave you alone. If someone should return before expected, I'll let you know."

He understood that she meant Glory. "I'd appreciate that."

An hour and a half later, he'd made a big dent in the mess that had been Abe Caldwell's workshop. He might have gotten more done if he hadn't become so absorbed in all the antique tools and hand-drawn designs he'd discovered. He could only imagine what other things might be hidden in the old building.

When he'd finished doing as much as he could, he placed the saddle stand in the middle of the cleared space, where it could be seen the minute anyone stepped into the big room. As he stood there looking at it, he felt a slow smile pulling his lips upward—the first he could remember in more years than he could count. No matter what happened, he would always feel good about giving Glory back her saddle.

On the drive home he thought about all that had happened over the past couple of months. He'd never believed anything good would happen. Not after the accident. He hadn't even cared. He'd dedicated his life to making the ranch that had been his father's family legacy a success.

And then Glory had returned to Desperation. He'd started thinking maybe he could care again, without fear. But he'd closed himself off for so long, he didn't know how to let her know how she made him feel. But in the end, he'd ruined that. He'd had to. Just the thought of losing her tore him apart. He hoped giving her the saddle would be the first step to at least repairing that.

The first thing he noticed when he pulled up to the ranch was that her car was gone. With the decorating nearly finished, if not finished already, he knew he wouldn't be seeing much of her. Missing her was only the tip of his feelings. Just thinking about that made him want to go to her and tell her that he loved her, even though he'd never meant for it to happen. But he couldn't do it. Still, there was a spark of hope he hadn't been able to destroy.

When he walked into the kitchen, he had the sense that something was different, but he couldn't put his finger on what it might be. Shrugging it off, he went through the dining room and climbed the stairs to his bedroom. A steaming shower put him in a good mood and after dressing in a pair of worn blue jeans and a T-shirt, he returned to the kitchen. It took a few minutes before he realized that there were plants on the windowsill above the sink, just like when he was a kid. A few colorful pictures were now hanging on the wall that hadn't been there before, either. Glory had been busy with what she called her "finishing touches," that was for sure.

With a grunt, he walked down the hall to the living room, intending to watch a little television before going to bed. Settling on the sofa, he grabbed the remote, ready to run through the evening's offerings, but slowly realized that the empty places in the shelves surrounding the wide-screen were now filled. Because the light was low in the room, he put down the remote, stood and went to see what new things Glory had added to the room.

But what he saw made him take a step back and wish he hadn't looked. Pictures he remembered from an old photo album that he hadn't seen for fifteen years were now displayed in frames. There was one of him and his dad, a grin on his face and a baseball hat on his head. Another photo was of his mother, his brother and sister and himself before a large and heavily decorated Christmas tree.

There'd been a reason he'd boxed up all the photos and put them in the attic. He hadn't wanted to deal with the memories and the pain they caused.

And now he was seeing it all again—the flashing lights of the police cars and ambulance arriving at the scene of the accident, the twisted metal of his parents' car, the cold wet of the rain. He heard himself cry out, but he didn't know if it was the memory or if it was real.

GLORY ENTERED THE shop, flipped the sign on the door to read Closed and locked the door. Sighing, she tossed her bag to the floor and collapsed in the old wing chair she'd insisted they keep instead of selling.

"Is that you, Glory?" her grandmother asked from the small office.

"A very tired me," Glory answered. Closing her eyes, she leaned her head back. Who would have thought that putting photos in frames and finding places for them could be so exhausting? If it hadn't been for Hayley, she'd still be working, with maybe half of it done. But the Walker house was finished, except for one last thing to do later, and that wouldn't take long.

"How did it go?" Louise asked, coming to stand beside the chair.

Glory looked up with a tired smile. "More work than I'd imagined, but I think it's all done."

"Good news, then." She reached behind her and untied the cotton apron knotted at her waist. "Has Dylan seen it?"

Shaking her head, Glory looked at her watch. "He wasn't home by the time I left, but he probably is by now. I'll check with him tomorrow to make sure everything is all right."

"You sound a little disappointed."

The last thing Glory wanted was for her grandmother to think there might be something between her and Dylan. While she sometimes wished there might be, she had no reason to believe it would happen. In fact, quite the opposite, which was just as well. She sometimes felt herself falling into the old trap of wanting to please. It was something she would have to watch closely when working with future clients.

"I think it's a combination of the letdown of finishing the job and being tired," she told her grandmother. "Hayley came and helped, so it went faster than it would have, and I really enjoyed her company."

"I've heard she's nice," Louise said. "We haven't met yet, though."

"She *is* nice."

"It's good you've made a new friend."

Nodding, Glory stood, rubbing a spot that ached in her back. "So many of my old friends have moved away."

"Oh, I think they're around. You just haven't had the opportunity to run into them. Now that you've finished the Walker house, I'm betting things will change."

Glory wasn't sure she cared. She needed to focus on her business. She had accepted that people change, find new interests and new friends. She and Kyle hadn't made many trips back. He'd always been tied up with business. At least that was what he'd always told her. She now knew it wasn't completely true.

"I found a few interesting things upstairs you might want to look at tomorrow," Louise said. "If you have time."

Glory stretched her arms over her head. "I'll make time."

"You really are tired. It might be good for you to call it a day and go on home early."

"I'm ready for a long, hot shower," Glory said, and started to walk away.

"Oh, wait," Louise said. "Would you mind doing something for me?"

Glory stopped and looked back. "Sure. What is it?"

Louise made a face and shook her head. "I took some things out to the workshop earlier and just remembered that I left my keys sitting on the workbench by the door. Would you mind getting them? While you do that, I'll turn off the lights in here."

"Of course," Glory answered. Although she didn't go out in the workshop often because it was a reminder of how much she missed her grandfather, she also understood that her grandmother felt the same, only more so. At the door that led into the workshop, she prepared herself for the sadness, and then opened the door.

The lights were off, and she had to reach to her left for the light switch. The fluorescent overhead lights flickered, then bathed the room in cool light. She looked on the workbench for her grandmother's keys, but had a strange feeling that something was different. Slowly turning her head to see what might be causing it, she noticed first that the workshop wasn't nearly as cluttered as it had been.

And then she saw it. Her saddle, the one her grandfather had made her when she was eight years old and she'd sold to Erin Walker, sat on one of the saddle stands in a cleared space in the middle of the room.

Thinking she must be imagining things, she carefully walked down the two steps into the room, praying it wasn't a mirage.

"Oh, it's real, sweetie," her grandmother said from behind her.

Stopping to stand next to the beautiful piece of leatherwork, Glory reached out and touched it. "Where did it come from?" she asked without turning around.

"Dylan brought it earlier. I believe he bought it from his sister."

With tears in her eyes and her heart aching with joy, Glory stroked the tooled leather with her fingertips. He'd bought it from his sister and returned it to her? That could only mean that he truly had some sort of feelings for her, didn't it?

Turning back to her grandmother, the words tumbled from her lips as she tried to hold back her happy tears. "I need to tell him thank you. Could you—"

"I'll lock up," Louise answered before she could even finish asking. "I'll put the casserole that's in the oven away for you so you can have a bite to eat when you get home."

"Don't wait up for me," Glory said, hurrying up the steps past her. "I won't be too—" She stopped and looked at the workbench. "I don't see your keys."

"Oh, I found them on that table by the chair," Louise said matter-of-factly.

Glory put her arms around her grandmother. "Thank you."

Louise hugged her close, and then moved away. "You'd better get going. He might decide to call it an early night. He worked pretty hard out here today."

Glory nodded and hurried through the shop, out to her car, and was gone. Ten minutes later, she opened the screen door of the porch, wondering how she could explain to Dylan how much the gift of her saddle meant to her. Inside, the kitchen was empty, so she walked down the short hallway to the living room, where a low light was burning in the corner. But no one was in the room, and she wondered if he might have already gone to bed. The thought of waiting until the morning filled her with disappointment, but she tried to cheer herself with the thought that she might get there in time to see his reaction to the gift she'd been working on for weeks and had set up that afternoon.

Scolding herself for being foolish and thinking she'd simply rush in and thank Dylan for the saddle, she turned to leave. As she started for the door, she heard a noise coming from his office. Of course! Why hadn't she thought of it?

Turning down the hallway, she called to him. "Dylan? It's Glory. I came to tell you—"

"Go away, Glory."

From the office doorway, she could see the banker's lamp casting shadows on the desk, where he sat with his arms crossed, his forehead resting on them. Fear gripped her, and she stepped into the room. "What's wrong, Dylan?"

"Just go away."

Knowing something wasn't right, she couldn't leave

him. She had to try to help him. "Dylan, please let
me—"

"What? Help?" He straightened in the chair and
raised his head. "You've already helped enough."

She had no idea what he was talking about, but her
heart pounded a warning. "I don't understand."

He turned to look at her. "Why did you do it?"

"Do what?" When he moved his arms, she noticed
the nearly empty bottle on the desk, along with the half-
full glass in his other hand. Disappointment cut through
her as she fought back the tears that threatened to fall.

"You tell me why you did it," he said, his words
slightly slurred as he struggled to his feet and faced her.
"All those pictures. Didn't you wonder why they were in
the attic? Don't you think that if I'd wanted them around
to remind me, I'd have left them all over the place?"

If she thought she'd hurt when he'd called their lovemaking a mistake, the look on his face proved she'd
never known real pain. "I didn't know," she said in a
whisper as she walked toward him. "I had no idea."

"Nobody does."

Before she reached him, he sank back down on the
chair. Knowing in her heart that she had to find a way
to help him, she knelt in front of him and took his hands
in hers. "You can tell me, Dylan. Whatever it is, you'll
feel better when you talk about what's hurting you."

He shook his head.

Tears spilled from her eyes. "Look at me, Dylan.
Whatever it is, you have to let it go."

His head came up and he stared at her with eyes full
of agony. "Let it go?" he said, pulling away and standing again. "My parents died because of me. How can
I let go of that?"

She couldn't believe what she was hearing. "It wasn't your fault. It was an accident."

"No. Don't you see?" He touched a finger to the scar above his eye. "It wouldn't have happened if they hadn't been on their way into town because I was at the doctor's office getting my head stitched."

"You didn't get hurt on purpose, Dylan."

His face hardened. "I should have gone straight home after the storm went through, but I didn't. Do you know what I was doing when I hit that tree? I was out mudding with some of the guys. Tearing up the back roads with the farm pickup, after I'd been warned not to. Doc Priller had his assistant call my parents while he put in the stitches because I wasn't eighteen yet."

"You were a kid, Dylan. A kid who, like every other high school boy, did things you shouldn't have. But it didn't cause your parents' accident. You have to believe that."

"Do you?"

"Of course I do."

"It was my fault."

Her breath caught at the intensity in his voice. "Let's go out—"

"I stood at that accident scene and swore I'd spend the rest of my life making the ranch a success. That's what they would have wanted me to do. And with Luke's help, it is a success. But they aren't here to see it. They aren't here."

With sudden clarity, she understood. "You miss them. It isn't the guilt. It's because you lost the people you loved."

He turned around and grabbed the glass off the desk. Lifting it to his mouth, he took a drink. "What?" he asked as she watched.

She stood her ground. "Let's go outside and get some fresh air. I'll take the pictures away and we'll talk."

"Nothing to talk about." He took another drink.

"That's not true. I care about you, Dylan. I—" She stopped, not sure if she should continue. The anger was gone and all that was left was her heart. There was nothing more she could do, except tell him.

She moved closer, until she was standing in front of him, and took the glass from his hand, setting it on the desk. "I didn't mean to fall in love with you, Dylan, but it happened. I understand now that those photos are a reminder of the loss of the people you loved, and you're afraid of getting close to people. Afraid of losing someone again."

"You don't know what you're talking about."

But she did, and she could see the truth in his eyes. "I know about loss, too. Things happen that we don't expect. Life happens. Death happens." She paused, and took a breath. "And love happens. Take the risk, Dylan."

Realizing she couldn't get through to him, she turned to leave. In the doorway, she looked back to see him slumped at the desk, his hands wrapped around the glass, and she suddenly understood the reason he'd worked so hard, yet kept to himself.

"You need to let go of the past, Dylan. You'll never be able to feel the good things, if you don't."

His answer was a shake of his head, and she walked away.

Chapter Eleven

It took Dylan two days to recuperate, then find and pack up all the photos Glory had framed and placed around the house. The entire time, he cussed himself for opening up to her. Somehow, she'd guessed the truth about him. To top it off, he'd told her what he'd been doing that day of the accident, something even his brother and sister didn't know. Now that he'd shocked Glory with the truth, he was torn between wishing he'd never said anything and feeling relief at having told her. Any crazy, foolish idea he'd even briefly entertained about having a future with her had come to a crashing end. And he'd made sure of it.

With two large boxes full of framed photos on the floor at his feet, he surveyed the living room. He never would have believed it could look the way it did now. It was as beautiful as Glory. And his mother would have loved it.

He squeezed his eyes shut, hoping to hold off the pain. The guilt over his parents' accident had always been a buffer, an excuse not to feel the pain of losing his parents. And now he'd intentionally pushed away the woman he loved.

"Where the hell have you been?"

Dylan spun around at the sound of his brother's

voice, nearly tripping over one of the boxes. "Here," he answered. "I've been here."

Luke walked into the room from the kitchen. "Is something wrong with your phone? I've been calling you since yesterday morning."

The day before was still hazy from the hangover, thanks to all he'd had to drink the night before. He'd never liked lying, but it was his only option. "I've been sick," he said, which wasn't far from the truth. "I shut it off."

Luke's eyes narrowed as he studied him. "Sorry to hear it, but I wish you'd given me a call to let me know. The vet was out checking on the herd yesterday morning, so I couldn't come by and check on you. Then I had things to do with Hayley."

"I slept most of the day," Dylan answered, adding to his dishonesty. "It was late last night when I finally crawled out of bed." At least that much was true, he thought.

"What's that?" Luke asked.

"What's what?" Dylan saw his brother nod toward the boxes at his feet. "Oh, those. Some pictures."

Luke moved closer. "Of what?"

Dylan shrugged and took a step away. "Us. Pop and Mama. Just old pictures."

"Yeah?" Luke leaned down and picked up a picture from one of the boxes, then grabbed another. "Where'd you find these? They weren't in these frames, were they? Because I kind of remember seeing some of them in an album."

"They were in the attic."

"So who put them in the frames?"

"She did."

"Glory did?"

Dylan nodded.

Smiling, Luke shook his head. "That was real nice of her. If you were smart, you'd—"

"There's something I need to tell you," Dylan said before Luke could say things he didn't want to hear.

Luke returned the photos to the box, straightened and looked Dylan square in the eye. "Oh, yeah? What's that?"

"I've decided to leave."

Luke's frown was almost menacing. "We've gone over this before, and I thought you had it all taken care of this spring. That's what you told me, remember?"

Dylan remembered, but none of that mattered now. "I won't be coming back."

"That's bull—"

"Maybe you can find somebody who'll rent the place or whatever, but I can't stay."

"Why not?"

Dylan couldn't tell him the truth that Glory had managed to guess, but his brother deserved some kind of explanation. "All this work she did—"

"She? You mean Glory?"

"Yeah. All this work and all the changes she made…" He shook his head.

"I thought you were doing better."

"I did, too." It was true. He'd even gotten to the point of thinking he might someday have a chance at a normal life. A life with Glory, if he was lucky. And then he'd seen all the pictures, and the enormity of what he'd lost had hit him like a sledgehammer. Erin had never understood. No matter how different new paint or new furniture made it look, his parents were still gone.

"You know," Luke said, his voice lowered, "I had a hard time living in my house for a while after Kendra left. There were too many memories—a lot of them bad. The marriage had been a mistake, and I had to admit it. Moving somewhere else wasn't an option. And then a few months later, I realized that Brayden and I were making new memories, and I didn't think a lot about the old ones."

"You were lucky," Dylan said. "You had Brayden, and now Hayley."

Luke put a hand on his shoulder. "You could be lucky, too. Give it a chance. Maybe Glory is the—"

Dylan pulled away. "No."

Luke opened his mouth to speak, but closed it, shaking his head.

"I'm sorry about this, Luke. I never meant to cause you any trouble."

"You're not trouble! I don't want you to leave. You're my brother, and I'm here for you, no matter what."

"But I can't stay here any longer."

Nodding, Luke stepped away. "Okay. But don't close yourself off to the possibility of some other option."

"Right."

Dylan followed his brother into the kitchen and then to where Luke's pickup was parked. Nothing was going to be easy, he knew, but at least he believed he was doing the right thing for himself and everybody else involved.

Luke climbed into the truck, started the engine and then rolled down his window. "I meant to ask you. What's that thing out by the windbreak?"

Dylan looked in the direction of the line of trees bordering the far north edge of the yard. "What thing?"

Luke pointed. "I only caught a glimpse of it, but there's something out there. Maybe somebody dumped something, but you might want to take a look."

Dylan nodded. "I'll do that."

"I'll see you later?"

"Sure. I'll come by your place in a little while." There was work to do before he could leave. The least he could do was help until then. After that, he knew Luke could handle the ranch on his own.

After watching Luke drive away, Dylan turned and started for the house, but before he reached it, he remembered he needed to check out whatever was out by the windbreak. After rounding the house, he could see something near the tree line, and he walked toward it. From a distance, it appeared to be large and light colored. Had someone dumped a refrigerator out there? But the closer he got, he realized that it was much larger than that, and he wasn't quite sure what to make of it.

As he drew near, his heart began to beat faster. He suspected Glory must have had something to do with it. When he finally came to a stop in front of the octagonal, white gazebo, he had no doubt of that.

A lump the size of Oklahoma lodged in his throat as he stepped onto the stone base where the gazebo stood. On one of the back posts, he saw what appeared to be a small iron plaque, and he walked closer to read it.

A Place of Peace and Love
In Loving Memory of David and Ann Walker

Leaning against the post, he pressed his head to it, squeezing his eyes shut in hope of stopping the sting of tears. For a moment he couldn't breathe, and when he finally could, he started to lower himself to the bench that rimmed the entire inside of the gazebo. He was almost seated when he realized there was a piece of paper tucked behind the plaque. With shaking fingers, he carefully removed it.

It was some time before he could gather the courage to open the note, and even then, his hands shook so badly that he had trouble unfolding it so he could read the handwritten message.

It's understandable that your memories of the past are filled with a sadness that many of us will never have to deal with, but you must never think you were the cause of anything bad. You're too good to have done something to cause anyone harm, even by chance. The ranch has always been your home, as it was your parents and your grandparents and great-grandparents before you. This gazebo, dedicated to the memory of your parents, is a special place, where bad memories are left behind and cannot hurt you, and where good memories can fill your heart. May you someday find the peace you deserve. — Glory

The words blurred as he thought of what it had taken for her to write the words after the things he'd said to her less than forty-eight hours before. He'd been brutal, when nothing that had happened had been her fault. Somehow he had to find a way to be the man she believed him to be. The man she'd said she loved. He'd find a way to put the past behind him, deal with the loss he would never forget and pay any price for her forgiveness and her love.

"Is THAT your phone ringing again?" Louise asked, stepping into the small office in the shop.

Glory nodded and tried to focus on the papers in

front of her, determined to keep her mind on work, instead of the ringing phone and especially the things that were tearing her apart inside.

"I'll get it." Louise reached for the cell phone. "Ignoring possible clients is no way to run a business." Staring at the phone in her hand, she pushed a button and then held it to her ear. "Glory Be Antiques and Decorating."

Even though she knew it wasn't Dylan calling— none of the numerous calls over the past four days had been—Glory still hoped as she listened to her grandmother's side of the conversation. Somehow, word about her decorating had spread like wildfire throughout the small town. It seemed everyone needed something new done to their home.

"Oh, I'm sure we can find a time for you tomorrow," Louise told the caller. With a smile that said she could handle anything, she reached over and pulled the new appointment book toward her. But her smile disappeared, and she glanced at Glory before continuing. "What about five? Is that too late?" The smile reappeared as she listened. "Oh, no, it's not too late for us. I was thinking it might be late for you." Nodding, she picked up a pencil from the desk. "Then I'll put you down for five, Hettie. And thanks so much for thinking of us."

Giving the disconnect button an exaggerated punch with her finger, she looked at Glory as if she'd won some kind of prize and set the phone on the desk. "Hettie wants to talk about some ideas for the Commune."

Glory closed her eyes. "You saw the schedule, Gram." Opening them, she tried not to let her frustration get the best of her. "If even half of those people decide to hire me, when do you think I'll be able to fit in a job at the Commune?"

Louise gave an indignant sniff. "Hettie Lambert is not only the most influential person in this town, but a dear friend."

Too tired to argue, Glory sighed. "I know, and I'm sorry. Of course I'll be happy to talk with Hettie and do whatever I can."

"I'm sorry, too." Louise sat on the chair across the desk from Glory. "I should be helping more."

"I expect it will settle down in a day or two."

"Why would it?"

Glory shrugged. "I don't know why so many people are calling, although I think Hayley might have something to do with it."

"What a sweet girl," Louise said. "I finally met her in the doctor's office when I stopped in for a new prescription for my arthritis. She said she would soon be a... Now, what was that word she used?"

"Physician Assistant."

"Paige O'Brien is an excellent doctor," Louise continued with a nod, "but the people in this town seem to work her to death. Why, did you know that she goes to all the school sports events? I don't believe Doc Priller ever did that. Not unless it was something special, anyway. I can't imagine how she manages to do so much."

Glory was only half listening as she thought of the many small changes that had occurred while she'd been away. Friends and classmates had grown up and now had jobs and families. Some had moved away, but new people had moved to Desperation to take their places. The new doctor was just one of them. Glory had been so busy, she'd only had a chance to be introduced, and she wanted to get to know some of them better. Kate had invited her to a regular get-together with her sister Trish and some of their friends, wives of some of the boys she'd gone to school with, but there'd been so little time.

"You look tired," Louise said, pulling Glory from her thoughts. "Maybe we should—" She stopped and stared at the ringing phone.

Glory reached for it and hit the button to silence it. "That takes care of that."

"Maybe it's time to put a regular phone in here. A business phone. With an extra line and an *answering machine*."

Glory laughed. "We'll get one with all the bells and whistles."

"I'll call the phone company first thing Monday morning."

"Thanks, Gram," she said with a smile. "I don't know what I'd do if you didn't take such good care of me."

"We take care of each other." Louise pulled the appointment book closer and peered at it. "You know, I think that's the first time I've seen you smile all week."

Glory wasn't sure how to answer, so she pressed her lips together and hoped her grandmother didn't notice.

"I would have thought that after seeing the saddle Dylan returned, the two of you would be riding every day."

Glory ducked her head. "He's busy."

"Is he? You seemed pretty happy when you found it and then hightailed out of here to thank him."

Feeling her grandmother's gaze on her, Glory settled for a shrug and avoided looking at her. She was afraid that if she did, she wouldn't be able to keep it together.

"What happened, Glory? Because something did."

"Nothing happened."

Louise grunted. "I may be an old woman, but I'm not blind. What's going on?"

Tempted to insist that everything was fine, Glory tried to think of a response. Instead, her chest tightened, making it hard to breathe, while the tears that were fighting to be free blocked her throat, threatening to choke her.

"He's—" she began, but couldn't finish. Knowing she couldn't tell anyone—not even Gram—what he'd revealed, she shook her head. "He's so hard on himself."

"He's shouldered a lot of responsibilities these past years."

"He's a good man." Glory raised her head and let the tears fall. "He doesn't believe it, but he is." Unable to dam her emotions, she cried, "I just don't know what to do."

Louise stood and circled the desk, wrapping her arms around Glory. "Go ahead and cry. Sometimes it's the one thing we *can* do. You'll feel better for it."

Shaking her head, Glory said, "But it won't change anything." And the tears fell faster.

"Let me get you a tissue," Louise said and disappeared.

Glory wished she hadn't said anything. From the moment she'd left Dylan at the ranch the night she'd found him in his office and poured out her heart, she'd been trying to act as if nothing had happened. But even though she couldn't keep her tears from falling, she knew she needed to take control of herself. Her business was the success she'd hoped for, so why wasn't she celebrating?

"Here you go," Louise said, returning to hand her a box of tissues.

When Glory finally had a solid grasp on her emotions, she took a deep breath, feeling a little better and able to at least stop crying. Pushing away from the desk, she stood. "Thanks, Gram. Maybe I should get up and do something."

She was almost out the door when her grandmother spoke. "You've fallen pretty hard."

Taken off guard, Glory wasn't sure she'd heard her right. "Fallen?"

"In love."

Staring at her, Glory tried to think of something to say that would put an end to any other questions. Instead, she answered with a nod. "How did you guess?"

Louise smiled and shrugged. "I remember your wedding day. You were everyone's idea of the blushing bride, but there was something missing. I didn't know what it was. Maybe it's something in your eyes that I've been seeing for the past month, or the glow you have now that you didn't have back then."

"It doesn't matter," Glory said, ready to step out of the room.

"Of course it matters, and don't you walk out on this conversation."

Glory hung her head. Gram would never let it rest. Looking over her shoulder, she said, "It won't work."

"Why not?"

There was nothing she could tell her grandmother that wouldn't lead to more questions. But maybe Gram would understand one thing. "He can't let go of his past. He's never gotten over the loss of his parents."

Instead of answering, Louise nodded. "That won't stop me from hoping."

Glory's only answer was a smile she didn't feel. Gram could hope all she wanted, but it wouldn't change anything. "Why don't I get us something to eat?"

"Why don't you do that and take it home?" Louise answered. "I'll lock up and meet you there."

"Sounds good to me."

Glory was hoping, too. The café was the busiest place in town on a Friday evening, and it wouldn't be unusual if Dylan stopped in for supper. After all, he was a bachelor, and she knew for a fact that he didn't do a lot of cooking. She wasn't ready to see him yet, but neither could she let that determine what she did and didn't do.

In her car, she started the engine and backed onto the street, thinking of how, over the past four days, she'd held her breath every time the phone rang, thinking it might be Dylan. She'd scribbled the note she'd left in the gazebo after leaving him in his office. At the time, she'd thought it might help him see things in a different way. Later, she realized how foolish that idea had been. Not that it mattered. There was no guarantee he'd even seen the gazebo, so it was all wishful thinking.

Putting the car into Drive, she blew out a breath and continued down the street. She needed to take her own advice and get on with her life. It wasn't as if she had time to feel sorry for herself. She had what she'd always wanted, didn't she?

"Are you finding everything?"

Dylan turned to see Fred Mercer walking toward him. "Just browsing," he said.

"Let me know if you need some help."

"Will do," Dylan answered, and then turned back to look out the big window of the hardware store. It was the perfect place for keeping an eye on the shop across the street. So perfect that he'd just seen Glory get in her car and drive down the street to park in front of the café. He didn't expect she'd be watching for him, so it was time to walk over to the shop and have a talk with her grandmother.

It wasn't that he wanted to talk to Louise Gardner so much, but he'd gotten the feeling that giving Glory back her saddle had won him some points. Whether that gave him an edge or not, only time and getting some questions answered would tell.

He knew now that he couldn't just sit around and feel sorry for himself. Since finding the note Glory had left him, he'd tossed out everything that even hinted at alcohol. Then he'd returned all the photos to the places where Glory had put them. Or he'd tried, anyway. He wasn't sure exactly where they'd all been.

And he'd thought about what she'd said. She was right that he hadn't moved on. And she'd been on target about his fear of losing more people he loved. Sure, he could promise to change, but he knew it would take more than that. If only he knew what and how. And that was where Louise Gardner came in.

After making sure Glory had gotten out of her car and was inside the café, he pulled his hat lower and walked out the door. Looking both ways and hoping nobody noticed him, he crossed the street. Before he stepped up onto the sidewalk in front of the antiques shop, he could see Glory's grandmother locking up, and he reached the entrance at the same time she did.

Smiling, she opened the door. "Can I help you with something, Dylan?"

"Yes, ma'am," he said, pulling off his hat. "Or I hope so, anyway."

"Glory just stepped out to pick up something to eat."

"Yes, ma'am. I saw her head that way."

Her eyes widened, and she pursed her lips, as if she had a secret. "Aha. Well, knowing that is a good thing. Why don't you come on in?"

"That's mighty nice of you. Thank you."

She held the door open, and then shut it behind him. "I'll just lock it, in case somebody doesn't see the Closed sign in the window."

"Oh. Yeah." He wondered if she meant him. "I saw that, but I—"

"It wasn't meant to keep you away."

He nodded. When she waved a hand, indicating that he should follow her, he did. Realizing he hadn't thought this through very well, he wasn't sure what to say. But when they reached the back of the shop, where she pulled up a chair and pointed at one for him, all he could do was hope that he would do something right for a change.

"We've been getting a lot of calls from prospective clients," she said, smoothing the apron she wore with her hands. "Have you had anything to do with that?"

Stunned by her blunt question, he could only shake his head. "No, ma'am," he managed to say, wishing that he could have said he did. "But I'm glad to hear it."

"Glory's a little overcome by how many people want her services."

"That's a good thing, right?"

"Yes, it is. But she doesn't seem to be as happy as I thought she would be."

"Oh." He hoped that was a positive sign for him. Not that he didn't want her to be happy. "Well..."

"Dylan, do you mind if I ask you a personal question?"

"No, I suppose—"

"Good. Now don't be nervous. It's really a simple question. Maybe not an easy one to answer, but a yes or no will suffice."

"Okay." He had the distinct urge to squirm in his chair, but he remained still.

She leaned forward, her blue eyes boring into him. "Do you love my granddaughter?"

He opened his mouth, but nothing came out. The question wasn't at all what he'd expected.

"Well, do you?"

What was the right answer?

The truth. Tell her the truth.

"Yes, ma'am, I do."

She smiled and leaned back in the chair. "Good. Excellent, in fact."

He was pleased she was happy, but it didn't solve his problem. "There's a problem, though."

"Why did I think there wouldn't be?" she said, looking heavenward. "Then let's you and me get it solved, all right?"

He nodded, even though he wasn't sure it was going to be that easy. "I guess I need to tell her."

Nodding, she smiled and leaned forward. "Even better, you need to *show* her."

"I don't think—"

"There's no thinking to it. You do it."

"But I don't know how. You see, I'm one of those confirmed bachelors you hear about. You know, the ones who've sworn never to marry. I guess they haven't met anyone like Glory."

She chuckled softly. "I suppose they haven't."

"You make it sound easy."

"It isn't."

"No, it isn't. There are things I need to deal with first. Things that happened a long time ago."

"Maybe you should just let them go," she said, watching him.

"I wish I could."

Nodding, she sighed. "I understand. I've lost loved ones, myself. It isn't easy to move on."

"Or not to worry it will happen again," he said.

Her smile said she understood. "But it has to be done."

It didn't solve his problem. He hadn't moved on; he wasn't going forward yet. He was working on that fear thing, but he couldn't say he was getting very far with it.

"I guess I'd better be going," he said.

"If it were me..." She looked at him, her direct gaze stopping him from moving. "The first thing you need to do is prove to her that you've let go of the past and are moving on. There must be something you can do. Find that, and then you can let her know that you're ready to open your heart to love."

Was that it? He wished he knew what it was he needed to do to prove he was putting the past behind.

With a heavy heart, he walked with her back to the door and, after checking to make sure Glory had left the café and wasn't anywhere around, he thanked her grandmother. He didn't want to tell her that he might as well give up, so instead he said, "I'll do what I can."

Once he was outside, he didn't look back. It was all up to him. He could ride a kayak through the most dangerous rapids and rappel down a mountainside, but putting the past behind and loving someone seemed impossible.

Chapter Twelve

Glory walked to the door with the next-to-last appointment of the day. "Thanks again for stopping in, Carrie."

"It was so good to see you again, Glory," the young woman said. "And you'll call me when you have an opening?"

"Of course." Glory opened the door and smiled at her. "I can't promise how soon that will be, so I hope you'll be patient."

The woman stepped out the door, but turned back again. "Oh, I will be. I'm just so excited about this. Thank you."

"Thank *you*. I'll be in touch," Glory said, her face hurting from all the smiling she'd been doing throughout the long day.

Once the prospective client was gone, Glory closed the door and turned away, her smile now a grimace. She felt bad that she'd shooed Carrie out the door so quickly after their appointment, but the woman had asked far too many personal questions while reminiscing about their high school days. All Glory wanted to do now was sit and think of nothing until Hettie Lambert arrived, but a look at her watch told her there wouldn't be time to relax. It was nearly five, and Hettie was always punctual.

In the small office, Glory pulled her brush from a desk drawer and ran it through her hair. Her mind whirled with all the work ahead of her, but when she caught a glimpse of herself in the antique mirror hanging on the far wall, she stopped.

When had she become a grown-up? When did those lines at the corners of her eyes appear? She was still a young woman, but at that moment, she felt as old as Gram.

Nothing seemed right. She should be giddy with happiness. Less than a week after she'd officially finished Dylan's house, she'd had over a dozen calls from people in the area asking if she could do some work for them. But something was missing, and it was something she wouldn't allow herself to think had anything to do with Dylan.

She finished her hair and left the office. From her favorite chair at the front of the shop, she could see out the large window that overlooked Main Street. It brought back memories, and she realized that, in the past, people had admired her for things that had been important to her father, not her. Now she was at the threshold of proving that there was more to her than cheerleading and wearing a crown.

When a car pulled up and parked in front of the building, and then Hettie got out of it, Glory stood and made sure her smile was welcoming. Not only did Hettie deserve a warm welcome, but Glory knew how important it would be if Hettie hired her for work to be done at the Commune.

Hettie reached the door and Glory opened it. "Right on time."

Hettie's smile was apologetic but bright. "I try. And I'm really sorry it's so late," she added as Glory led her to the office. "I'm sure you'd like to be at home in a dark room with a cold cloth on your forehead."

Indicating with a nod that Hettie should go into the office ahead of her, Glory laughed. "Do I look that bad?"

"A little tired is all." She settled on the chair in front of the desk, while Glory walked around to take her own seat. "I'll get right to the point," Hettie said. "I've been hearing such good things about your work. Not that I'd have any doubt that you'd do anything that wasn't superb. You've always had many talents."

Embarrassed, Glory looked down at her hands, which were clasped on the desk. "Thank you, Hettie. That means a lot. So what is it you're thinking of doing at the Commune?"

Hettie tipped her head to the side. "You know, that old building is well over a hundred years old. Both my daddy and his daddy were born there and lived in it until they died. At the time I handed it over to Ernie to serve as a retirement home for the community, it was completely furnished."

"It's a beautiful place," Glory said. "I've always enjoyed going there to visit. And that decor you're talking about is classic. Pure antique."

Hettie nodded. "Oh, I know it is. But while there are a lot of memories in many of those things for me, that decor is beginning to show a lot of wear. I'd like to not only update the common rooms, but also give it a feel of openness." She leaned forward. "I don't know the correct terms. Never paid much attention. Am I explaining myself well?"

Glory felt the same exhilaration she'd felt when Erin had asked her if she'd be willing to do something with the Walker house. When Dylan had reluctantly agreed, she'd been over the moon. For good reason. Both structures had stood the test of time. She only wished she'd been around when the Opera House had been renovated.

"I can honestly say that I think I can help," she answered.

Leaning back, Hettie smiled. "I've heard such good things about what you did with Dylan Walker's house that I—"

"From whom?" Glory didn't doubt there'd been talk. Why else had there been so many people calling? "I'm sorry for interrupting, but I can't imagine Dylan saying anything. He simply isn't the type."

Hettie's bigger smile hinted that there were secrets behind it. "It only takes one person to start spreading the news, especially here in Desperation. You should remember that."

Glory nodded, thinking of the past. "Yes, good or bad, word travels fast."

"Speaking of which, I've heard a rumor that someone from the local paper will be calling you for an interview," Hettie said with a conspiratorial wink.

Glory could hardly believe what she was hearing, but she doubted Hettie would have mentioned it if it wasn't true. "That would be... *Wow.*"

"You've been a favorite in Desperation for a long time, Glory. People didn't forget you just because you were gone."

Thinking about how she'd come to this moment in time, Glory pushed away the bad memories and smiled. "It's something I've thought about doing for a long time. And I wanted to come back here to do it." She remembered Dylan's face when he saw his bedroom, but refused to think about anything more than that. "I love doing it."

"You've always been a sweet girl." Hettie reached across the desk and put her hand on Glory's. "And you obviously enjoy making people happy."

Nodding, Glory smiled. "Yes, I guess I do. Making people happy makes me happy."

"Does that mean you'll take the job?"

For a moment, Glory stared at her, and then she laughed. "Of course! In fact, I'm putting it first on the list. Hopefully all the others will understand."

"I'm sure most of them will, and those who don't, well, they'll get used to it or not have the pleasure of having you do the work."

But Glory was only half listening. What was it she'd said to Hettie? Making people happy made her happy? Closing her eyes, she took a deep breath, and then opened her eyes to look at Hettie, who didn't appear to notice that something might be wrong.

Before she could even think of something to say, there was a soft knock on the door. "Come in," she said.

The door opened, and her grandmother stood in the doorway. "I saw your car outside, Hettie," Louise said, "and I'm curious to know what you think about my granddaughter's work."

"I think you have a very talented granddaughter," Hettie said, standing. She turned to Glory, who also stood. "I don't want to keep you any later. Give me a call next week, and we'll go over the details."

"Yes, that sounds good," Glory said.

"I'll walk you to the door," Louise said.

When both women were gone, Glory sank back to the chair, her heart aching at what she'd been thinking before her grandmother had come in.

She'd spent her entire life trying to please everyone, and she'd done whatever it took to do it, no matter at what cost to herself. She was and had always been a people pleaser. As a child, she'd done everything she could to please her father. Then later her life had revolved around Kyle and his needs and wants. Until that moment, she hadn't realized that she'd given away her happiness. It was time to choose the things that made *her* happy.

In the back of her mind, she wanted Dylan to be a part of her life. But she'd ruined even that. Happiness might not be so easy to find.

"THE FOURTH OF July celebration is coming up next week," Luke said.

With his hands in the engine of the utility tractor and his mind on things it shouldn't be, Dylan grunted. "So I hear."

"Are you going?"

Dylan knew he couldn't let his guard down. Luke knew him too well, and if he didn't follow the usual script, there'd be some explaining to do. He didn't want to explain anything. How could he? He was still grappling with what Louise Gardner had said to him.

"I haven't really thought about it," he answered. "Hand me that torque wrench, will ya?"

"Here you go. You know, it's getting close to lunchtime. Want to run into town with Brayden and me? You know how he likes it when his uncle Dylan comes along."

Dylan wasn't ready to risk seeing Glory. "Not today. I want to get this finished."

"It can wait." When Dylan didn't answer, Luke sighed. "Okay, then I'm out of here. If you want to stay here and work on that, go ahead. I'm going to spend my time with my son. I'll see you later."

"Yeah."

Dylan waited until he heard the sound of Luke's pickup start and drive away. When all was quiet and he felt safe, he put down the tools, picked up a rag and wiped the grease from his hands.

Louise Gardner's words whispered in his mind as he walked to the house and went inside. *The first thing you need to do is prove to her that you've let go of the past and are moving on.*

If only he knew how to do that, but he'd spent the night before and all that morning trying to think of something—anything—that might work. So far, he'd come up empty-handed.

The shades were pulled down in his office, and he didn't bother to turn on the light when he walked in and made his way to his desk. There was no need. He had the room memorized, just like he'd memorized the last words Glory had said to him before she'd left him there, six days before. The note she'd written and left in the gazebo lay open on his desk, but he didn't bother to glance at it. He'd memorized it, too. And still he didn't know how he could prove he was leaving the past behind.

And he was. Slowly. He was doing his best to forget about the day that had changed all their lives and to not be afraid to love someone. If Glory had faith that he could do that, why didn't he have half as much in himself?

A framed photo of his high school baseball team sat on his desk, and he reached for it. He hadn't seen it for years, until Glory had discovered the box of photos he'd hidden in the attic. Now that he was over the shock of seeing all the photos again, he'd discovered that the sight of them didn't bother him. In fact, he had come to the point where he enjoyed seeing them. There was a new photo on the desk, too, one Erin had taken before she left and sent him only two days ago. In it, he and Luke were holding Brayden between them. Brayden and Luke were laughing, but he wasn't. That wasn't how he wanted his nephew to remember him.

On the other corner of his desk was the photo from the living room of him and his dad. Leaning back in his chair, he remembered that his dad had never missed one of his games. Had Glory known that? Had she realized the power the photos held for him? He believed that giving them to him had been her way of helping him heal, but he hadn't realized it until now.

He'd vowed never to play baseball again and hadn't. But what would happen if he did? Could he do it? And if he did, would it be proof enough that he was moving on?

When he heard his brother's voice calling his name, he looked at the clock on his desk. Over an hour and a half had passed since Luke had left.

"I'm in here," he called out.

"I thought you'd still be out working on the tractor," Luke said from the doorway of the office.

"I had some things to do." Dylan pushed away from the desk and stood. He felt strange, but it wasn't a bad feeling. He felt good, as if he'd found an answer he'd been seeking for a long time.

"Going back to work on the tractor?" Luke asked as he followed Dylan into the kitchen.

"Not today. I'm going upstairs to clean up and then run an errand."

Luke followed him to the stairs. "What's going on? You were so determined to get that tractor fixed."

With his foot on the first step, Dylan turned back. "Some other time."

An hour later he was at the O'Brien ranch, where he found Tucker O'Brien and his son Shawn working with some horses in the corral. Taking a deep breath, Dylan approached them, stopping at the fence.

"Hey, Dylan," Tucker called to him. "What brings you here?"

"I'd like to talk to Shawn, if that's okay."

Tucker glanced at his son, and then nodded at Dylan. "Sure. I'll just leave you two—"

"No need to do that. Your input is always welcome."

While Tucker tied the horses to the fence on the other side of the corral, Shawn joined Dylan and asked, "Is there something I can do for you?"

Dylan said what he'd practiced as he drove to see them. "I hear you're looking for some players for the baseball game on Thursday."

Shawn looked behind him at Tucker, whose eyebrows raised slightly as he walked toward them. Turning back to Dylan, Shawn said, "As a matter of fact, we could use one or two more. Do you know somebody who might want to play?"

"Maybe." Dylan watched as Shawn looked to his dad again. "One person, anyway."

"Yeah?" Shawn's eyes held a hint of anticipation. "Got a name?"

Hoping this was the right thing to do, Dylan shrugged. "I thought I might give it a try." When Shawn stared at him, saying nothing, Dylan wasn't sure if the young man understood. "If you don't mind a guy who hasn't caught or thrown a ball for fifteen years, that is."

"You? *You?* I don't believe—" Shawn's smile seemed to reach from ear to ear, and then he laughed. "Yeah. Oh, yeah, we'd love to have you on the team. You're a legend around these parts."

"Not hardly," Dylan answered. He'd never taken well to praise.

Tucker stuck his hand out, and Dylan took it. "Yeah, you are," Tucker said. "Don't sell yourself short."

"A small legend, then," he admitted with reluctance. "But I'm going to need some practice. A lot of it."

"Sure!" Shawn's eagerness shone in his eyes. "I mean, whenever you want, I'm available. Some of the other guys, too. We have a practice planned for tomorrow afternoon at two. If you can make it, of course."

"I'll make it." Just saying it made Dylan feel good.

"You have a mitt, right?"

Dylan nodded. He'd hidden it away in the loft in the barn and never looked at it again. "It's probably pretty stiff right now, but I think I can get it in shape with some oil and a good workout."

"Great. Then I'll see you tomorrow at the baseball diamond at the high school."

For a second, Dylan nearly backed out, wondering if he could handle the memories. Instead, he nodded and took the hand Shawn offered. "Tomorrow at the high school."

Heading back home in his truck, he pulled out his cell phone and hit an autodial number. "You'd better be home next Thursday," he said.

"I have things to do," Erin replied with an indignant sniff.

"I'm serious, Erin. I need you to be here."

For a moment, there was silence. "All right. But why?"

He felt the smile coming on. Even if this failed where Glory was concerned, he knew it was the right thing to do. Somehow he'd found a way to use the past to move forward.

GLORY WALKED THROUGH the park, surrounded by rides and booths selling everything from food to crafts and more. "I'd almost forgotten how much fun celebrating the Fourth of July in Desperation could be. This was always my favorite part of summer. How about you?"

Kate grinned. "Oh, it's definitely my favorite."

Having heard the story of how Dusty had chased Kate through town during the annual celebration and roped her so he could propose, Glory laughed, and then sighed. "I suppose it's because I haven't been here for so long. More than anything, it's getting to see people I hadn't thought of for years. And the memories it brings back, too, I guess."

"Good ones, I hope," Kate said. "And look, there's my sister, heading this way."

Trish shook her head when she joined them. "It's totally crazy over there at the refreshment stand. You'd think no one's had a bit of sugar for months. But look who I found."

Erin's grin was visible from several yards away, along with the four cones of cotton candy she was carrying. "Now I remember why I stopped coming back home for these," she called to them, pulling her mouth down in a make-believe frown.

Glory laughed as Erin drew closer. "And here I was just telling Kate how much I was enjoying this."

Trish relieved Erin of one of the sticky confections. "Don't believe what she says. Erin was enjoying all the attention she was getting."

"Was not," Erin said, lifting her chin as she handed a cotton candy to Glory. "It's just difficult to get away from people sometimes."

"I didn't know you'd planned to come back this soon," Glory said.

"I hadn't." Erin shrugged and smiled. "Plans change."

"How long will you be here this time?"

"I haven't decided. And if we don't hurry, we're going to be late."

Glory glanced at each of them. "Late for what?"

Kate, talking to Trish, looked at them. "Oh, didn't we tell you? Dusty and Morgan have decided to risk broken bones this afternoon."

"Doing what?"

"Playing baseball," Trish answered.

"Really? I don't remember Dusty playing in high school. He was too absorbed in rodeo and bull riding."

Kate nodded. "He was, but he was determined to be a part of this, so I guess he knows what he's doing."

Trish nodded. "All Morgan ever wanted to do was be a cop like his grandfather, but, like Dusty, he decided he was going to play. Why don't you two come with us to the game?"

Glory wasn't sure, but she did want to spend time with her friends. "It would be nice to sit for a while, I guess. I haven't walked this much since I don't remember when." She turned to Erin. "How about you?"

"I suppose it can't hurt."

Ten minutes later, they were entering the gate of the high school baseball field. "This brings back some memories," Glory said as they stepped inside the enclosure.

"Good ones?" Kate asked.

"I try to make all of them good," Glory answered with a smile.

"Let's find a seat," Erin said, and led them to the visitors' side of the field.

Glory pointed to a group of players throwing baseballs on the other side of the diamond. "Is that the high school team?"

"That's them," Kate answered. "I heard they won most of their games this year. Which doesn't bode too well for the old guys."

"Don't say that in front of Morgan," Trish said, laughing, "although he has been complaining of aches and pains in places he didn't know existed."

Their laughter was interrupted by the arrival of Jules O'Brien and her sister-in-law, Dr. Paige O'Brien. "I don't see our team," Jules said, sitting on the bleacher seat behind them. "Have they decided to forfeit?"

Kate shook her head. "They're over on the football field, warming up. Personally, I think they want to make a grand entrance."

"As long as they make an entrance," Jules replied.

Erin turned around. "Is Tanner playing?"

Jules tipped her head back and laughed. "Oh, heavens no! But he *is* coaching."

"Tucker isn't playing, either," Paige said, "but only because I put my foot down. His leg is stronger, but I don't want him taking a chance with it. He will, however, be on the bench, just in case he's needed."

"Nikki and Mac wanted to be here," Jules said, "but it was the only time they could get into a special seminar in Arizona. I'm sure next year will be different."

Glory turned to Kate. "Nikki?"

Kate nodded. "Tucker and Tanner's sister."

"They have a sister?" When Kate nodded, Glory shook her head. "I've missed so much."

"Don't worry," Erin said. "We'll get you up-to-date."

Blown away by all the things she hadn't known about, she turned her attention to the field. "You know,

I don't remember baseball games on the Fourth of July when I was in high school."

"It was Shawn's idea," Paige said. "He was on the high school team, but graduated last year. He's been itching to play some of his former younger teammates, so he decided to put together a team of 'old guys,' as he put it."

Kate laughed. "And very well put, I'd say."

Out of the corner of her eye, Glory caught sight of a group of ballplayers entering the home-team dugout. "Looks like our team has arrived. And don't those uniforms look nice!"

Jules nodded. "Gerald Barnes and a few others got together and bought the shirts and hats. The players paid for the rest."

"Maybe they'll make a habit of this."

"That remains to be seen, and only if they all survive," Jules said, laughter in her voice.

Shading her eyes against the bright afternoon sun, Glory tried to see who was on the team, but with all the players in uniform, she couldn't tell one from the other.

Erin touched her shoulder. "I'm going to get us something to drink." She looked at the others. "Is anyone else thirsty?"

While Erin took orders, Glory turned her attention back to the players as they took the field for a final warm-up before the game started. Just when she started to ask Kate which one of the players was Dusty, she stopped.

"It can't be," she whispered. "Erin, is that—" But Erin had left her seat.

Looking back toward the field, Glory's heart beat a little faster. The player she'd only seconds ago thought might be Dylan was now smiling at one of his teammates. Dylan didn't smile. But as she continued to watch, there was no doubt the player who was hustling to the dugout was Dylan.

And he was *smiling*.

Around her, the other women chatted about the players and other things, but Glory barely heard them. When did Dylan decide to join the team? Why hadn't he told her? But more important, why had he done it?

As she watched the team take the field to start the game, she felt certain he hadn't been forced into playing. His smile was genuine and he appeared to be enjoying himself completely. What had happened to change things?

Erin returned, but Glory barely noticed, too wrapped up in what was going on out on the field. She couldn't stop smiling each time Dylan went to bat or made a play in the infield. Before long, she didn't care why he was there, only that she couldn't remember being so happy.

Although they were trailing behind one run in the last inning, being the home team gave the "old guys" one last chance at bat. With Dusty on second base, thanks to a steal after a walk, Morgan stepped up to the plate, and the stands grew quiet. But the look of determination on his face grew grim after he'd watched two strikes go by him. The outcome of the game didn't look good for the home team.

At the next pitch, the crack of the bat hitting the ball sounded like a firecracker, and the crowd was on its feet. Erin grabbed Glory on one side, while Kate grabbed her from the other, and Trish yelled. "Run, Morgan, run!"

But Morgan hadn't reached first base before it was clear there was no need to run. The ball soared over the center-field fence, leaving the outfielders staring. First

Dusty rounded third base and scored, and then Morgan followed, coming to a stop on home plate, where the team joined him to pound him on the back and head, then doused him with a large cooler of water.

It wasn't Morgan whom Glory stood watching. Her heart filled with joy at the smile on Dylan's face as the players continued to congratulate each other. She couldn't drag her attention away and wondered how long it had been since he'd allowed himself to be happy.

He must have felt her watching him, because his gaze caught hers and held it. For a moment she stopped breathing. She watched as he tipped his head in the direction of the gate and then pointed to it. Taking a deep breath, she nodded.

The wives around her were leaving the bleachers to join the players, and she followed. But instead of walking onto the field with them, she slipped away. Moving along the back side of the bleachers and headed for the gate, she lost sight of Dylan. Hoping she hadn't mistaken his signal, she gasped when someone grabbed her around her waist. Before she knew it, she'd been pulled up against a hard, muscled chest, and was looking up into a pair of familiar green eyes.

"We won," he said.

"Yes," she breathed. "And you're smiling."

He nodded. "I have a lot to smile about."

"I'm glad."

"Me, too."

For a moment they simply looked at one another, until Dylan leaned closer. Every bone in her body turned to liquid when their lips met, and her head spun with a dizziness she'd never experienced. This was what it felt like to be kissed by someone she loved, and she hoped it would never end.

"Looks like I wasn't the only one to get a home run."

Startled by the voice coming from behind her, Glory moved to step out of Dylan's arms, but he held her close. She both heard and felt his soft laughter, and he kissed her again.

A new voice called out. "Why don't you two meet us at Lou's, whenever you can tear yourselves away from each other."

"Hush, Dusty."

"Kate, honey, I don't want them to miss the celebration."

"I think they need to enjoy their own celebration. Now, come on."

Wrapped up in Dylan's kiss, Glory barely heard the others pass on by. When the two of them finally came up for air, she giggled like a schoolgirl. "I don't believe I've ever been kissed under the bleachers until now."

He watched her, his eyes dark with passion. And with love. "I'm glad I could be the first."

"I am, too."

His chest rose and fell as he took a deep breath. "I'm ready to take the plunge."

She didn't understand. "Excuse me?"

"The plunge," he said, smiling. "I love you, Glory. I think I have since we were kids. I was just...afraid. Afraid that if I loved you, I might lose you. Afraid that you wouldn't want me—"

"Hush." She reached up and stroked the scar above his eye with a finger.

Taking her hand in his, he kissed her finger. "But there's one more thing."

For a moment, she felt afraid, but she pushed the fear away. "All right."

"Marry me, Glory."

Speechless, she pressed her hand to the hard angles of his face until she found her voice. "I love you, Dylan, with all my heart. And I'd love to be your wife."

Smiling, he placed a kiss in her palm. "That's all I need."

In the distance, she heard a horn honk. "I think the natives are restless."

"They're never going to give us any peace. You know that, right?"

"It's okay," she said, "as long as I have you."

Epilogue

The evening air had a definite chill to it, but Dylan blamed it on the arrival of September, only days before. An unexpected cool front had the weather feeling more like fall than the summer they'd just left behind. And what a summer it had been. He almost hated to see it end. In his memory it would always be the summer when Glory taught him how to love.

Looking across the O'Briens' patio, he caught her eye, smiled and shrugged. Their friends were throwing them an engagement party, but he couldn't figure out why he and Glory had barely had a chance to spend ten seconds with each other since they'd arrived.

He'd spent more time with friends over the past two months than he had in the previous fifteen years. He enjoyed being with them, but he'd rather spend time alone with the woman he loved.

"You didn't know you had so many friends, did you?" Luke asked, stopping to stand beside him.

Tearing his gaze from the woman he would spend the rest of his life with, Dylan looked at his brother, ready to point out that most of the people there had been friends for as long as he could remember. But it was clear that Luke was ribbing him. After all, until Glory walked into his life, he hadn't done much socializing.

"Good friends," he answered. And he was grateful for each and every one of them.

Beside him, someone chuckled, and he turned to see Tucker. "I know exactly what you're feeling," Tucker said. "You finally find a woman you want to spend your life with, and everybody finds a way to keep you apart. Happens to all of us."

"You, too, huh?" Dylan asked and laughed. "At least I'm in good company."

"Great company," Tucker said.

"The best." Dylan had only begun to realize everything he'd missed by keeping to himself. That wouldn't happen again. Even if he tried, Glory would pull him back into the here and now with a kiss.

The ring of metal tapping crystal caught their attention and they turned to see his sister, her smile as big as Texas. When everyone was quiet, she laughed. "Good golly, I do have a way of getting attention, don't I?"

"It sure isn't your pint size," Dusty said from somewhere behind Dylan.

While everyone laughed, Erin gave him a look that earned her his famous grin. "I'd like to make a toast," she said, ignoring him, "so y'all need to fill up the kids' cups with juice and your glasses with champagne, and find your special honey to share this with."

The grown-ups scrambled to make sure the eight children, ranging in age from two years old to ten, had their own cups for toasting. Dylan found Glory and slipped his arm around her waist, pulling her close.

"It's a beautiful night," she said.

"Not nearly as beautiful as you," he answered, still amazed at his good fortune.

When everyone was ready, Erin continued. "There have been several special moments in my life, and most of them involve my little brothers. I couldn't be prouder of both of them. Together we made it through the worst times to come out even better than before. And that's what we're celebrating today."

The sounds of the evening could be heard as everyone seemed to take a moment to look back at the past and catch up with the present. Dylan felt a familiar sadness, but the pain of losing his parents had become easier every day. He was moving on and making a new life for himself and Glory to share.

When Erin spoke again, her voice was husky with emotion. "I'm especially proud of my brother Dylan for finding a woman who suits him so well, and I'm tickled to say she'll soon be my sister. Would you all join me in showing our love and friendship to two very special people?" She turned and raised her glass to the couple. "To Dylan, who shouldered more responsibility than a boy his age should have, but came out a man with a heart full of love. And to Glory, who tells me she's more than ready to exchange her Prom Queen crown for a wedding veil. I couldn't be happier for both of them."

Luke, standing with Hayley, raised his glass. "To Dylan and Glory, two very special people who, though they were resistant at first, have had the good fortune to fall in love with each other. May your lives be filled with love and laughter."

A chorus of congratulations went up from the friends, and Dylan was touched by the warmth of their friendship and good wishes. "We sure have some good friends," he whispered to Glory, adding a quick kiss behind her ear.

"None better," she agreed, her eyes glowing with love.

Friends began to surround them, but Erin beat them all. "So when is the wedding?"

Glory looked from her to Dylan, who shrugged. "We really haven't set a date."

Erin glanced over her shoulder at Luke. "What about you two? Have you and Hayley picked a day?"

Hayley shook her head. "Not really, but we will soon, now that the date has been set for the ground breaking of the new hospital."

Nodding, Erin smiled. "Just as I thought. So what would you all think of a double wedding?"

Dylan noticed that Glory's eyes were wide with surprise, and Luke and Hayley seemed to be considering the idea.

"That's not a bad idea," Hayley said.

"I think I'd like to share my wedding and anniversaries with my new brother and sister," Glory agreed.

As everyone began to offer suggestions, Dylan stepped back and watched. He never thought he'd experience the kind of happiness he felt at that moment, and he wondered if it could ever be matched. Somehow, he thought it just might be, as he shared the rest of his life with Glory.

She joined him, slipping her arm through his. "Do you think we could escape for a few minutes? I need some alone time with you."

Dylan couldn't stop his smile. "I was thinking the very same thing. I have a feeling life just took a turn toward crazy."

"Do you mind?"

Pulling her into his arms, he looked at her. "No, I don't mind, but it's going to be more than a few minutes." He didn't care who was around—he kissed her with all the love he'd denied himself for too many years. He had no doubt his parents were looking down on them, smiling, and that maybe they'd even had a hand in getting them together.

"They'll always be with us," Glory whispered when the kiss ended.

He nodded. "I guess it's just part of life's design. And I'm glad you're a part of it. Forever."

* * * * *

COMING NEXT MONTH
from Harlequin® American Romance®

AVAILABLE JULY 1, 2013

#1457 BRANDED BY A CALLAHAN
Callahan Cowboys
Tina Leonard
Dante Callahan never dreamed that the nanny he's had his eye on has her eyes on him. But when Ana St. John seduces him, Dante's determined to make her his!

#1458 THE RANCHER'S HOMECOMING
Sweetheart, Nevada
Cathy McDavid
Sam Wyler returns to Sweetheart, a storybook place for eloping couples, to breathe new life into the town and win back Annie Hennessy—if she can only forgive him for his sins of long ago.

#1459 THE COWBOY NEXT DOOR
The Cash Brothers
Marin Thomas
Cowboy Johnny Cash has always thought of Shannon Douglas as a little sister. But when they bump into each other at a rodeo, the lady bull rider seems all grown-up...and just his type!

#1460 PROMISE FROM A COWBOY
Coffee Creek, Montana
C.J. Carmichael
When new evidence surfaces from an old crime, rodeo cowboy B. J. Lambert finally returns home. Not to defend himself, as Sheriff Savannah Moody thinks—but to protect *her*.

You can find more information on upcoming Harlequin® titles, free excerpts and more at www.Harlequin.com.

HARCNM0613

REQUEST YOUR FREE BOOKS!
2 FREE NOVELS PLUS 2 FREE GIFTS!

 HARLEQUIN®

LOVE, HOME & HAPPINESS

YES! Please send me 2 FREE Harlequin® American Romance® novels and my 2 FREE gifts (gifts are worth about $10). After receiving them, if I don't wish to receive any more books, I can return the shipping statement marked "cancel." If I don't cancel, I will receive 4 brand-new novels every month and be billed just $4.74 per book in the U.S. or $5.24 per book in Canada. That's a savings of at least 14% off the cover price! It's quite a bargain! Shipping and handling is just 50¢ per book in the U.S. and 75¢ per book in Canada.* I understand that accepting the 2 free books and gifts places me under no obligation to buy anything. I can always return a shipment and cancel at any time. Even if I never buy another book, the two free books and gifts are mine to keep forever.

154/354 HDN F4YN

Name   (PLEASE PRINT)

Address   Apt. #

City   State/Prov.   Zip/Postal Code

Signature (if under 18, a parent or guardian must sign)

Mail to the Harlequin® Reader Service:
IN U.S.A.: P.O. Box 1867, Buffalo, NY 14240-1867
IN CANADA: P.O. Box 609, Fort Erie, Ontario L2A 5X3

Want to try two free books from another line?
Call 1-800-873-8635 or visit www.ReaderService.com.

* Terms and prices subject to change without notice. Prices do not include applicable taxes. Sales tax applicable in N.Y. Canadian residents will be charged applicable taxes. Offer not valid in Quebec. This offer is limited to one order per household. Not valid for current subscribers to Harlequin American Romance books. All orders subject to credit approval. Credit or debit balances in a customer's account(s) may be offset by any other outstanding balance owed by or to the customer. Please allow 4 to 6 weeks for delivery. Offer available while quantities last.

Your Privacy—The Harlequin® Reader Service is committed to protecting your privacy. Our Privacy Policy is available online at www.ReaderService.com or upon request from the Harlequin Reader Service.

We make a portion of our mailing list available to reputable third parties that offer products we believe may interest you. If you prefer that we not exchange your name with third parties, or if you wish to clarify or modify your communication preferences, please visit us at www.ReaderService.com/consumerchoice or write to us at Harlequin Reader Service Preference Service, P.O. Box 9062, Buffalo, NY 14269. Include your complete name and address.

HAR13R

SPECIAL EXCERPT FROM

H HARLEQUIN

Looking for another great Western read?
Read on for a sneak peek of

THE RANCHER'S HOMECOMING

by Cathy McDavid

July's Harlequin
Recommended Read!

*Annie Hennessee has her hands full with
rebuilding the Sweetheart Inn following a
devastating forest fire. But what is Sam Wyler
doing back in town? Isn't it enough that he
broke Annie's heart all those years ago?*

A figure emerged from the shadows. A man. He wore jeans and
boots, and a black cowboy hat was pulled low over his brow.

Even so, she instantly recognized him, and her broken heart
beat as if it was brand-new.

Sam! He was back. After nine years.

Why? And what was he doing at the Gold Nugget?

"Annie?" He started down the stairs, the confused expression
on his face changing to one of recognition. "It's you!"

Suddenly nervous, she retreated. If he hadn't seen her, she'd
have run.

No, that was a stupid reaction. She wasn't young and vulnerable
anymore. She was thirty-four. The mother of a three-year-old
child. Grown. Confident. Strong.

And yet the door beckoned. He'd always had that effect on her,
been able to strip away her defenses.

A rush of irritation, more at herself than him, galvanized her.

HAREXP0713

"What are you doing here?"

Ignoring her question, he descended the stairs, his boots making contact with the wooden steps one at a time. Lord, it seemed to take forever.

This wasn't, she recalled, the first time he'd kept her waiting. Or the longest.

At last he stood before her, tall, handsome and every inch the rugged cowboy she remembered.

"Hey, girl, how are you? I wasn't sure you still lived in Sweetheart."

He spoke with an ease that gave no hint of those last angry words they'd exchanged, and he even used his once-familiar endearment for her. He might have swept her into a hug if Annie hadn't stepped to the side.

"Still here."

"I heard about the inn." Regret filled his voice. "I'm sorry."

"Me, too." She lifted her chin. "We're going to rebuild. As soon as we settle with the insurance company."

"You look good." His gaze never left her face. She was grateful he didn't seem to notice her khaki uniform, rumpled and soiled after a day in the field. Or her hair escaping her ponytail and hanging in limp tendrils. Her lack of makeup.

"Th-thank you."

"Been a while."

"Quite a while."

His blue eyes transfixed her, as they always had, and she felt her bones melt.

Dammit! Her entire world had fallen apart the past six weeks. She didn't need Sam showing up, kicking at the pieces.

Will Sam turn out to be a help or a hindrance to Annie's attempts to rebuild her life?

Find out in THE RANCHER'S HOMECOMING by Cathy McDavid, book one of her new SWEETHEART, NEVADA trilogy.

Available in July 2013, only from Harlequin American Romance.

Copyright © 2013 by Cathy McDavid

HAREXP0713

SADDLE UP AND READ 'EM!

This summer, get your fix of Western reads and pick up a cowboy from the HOME & FAMILY category in July!

BRANDED BY A CALLAHAN by Tina Leonard,
Callahan Cowboys
Harlequin American Romance

THE RANCHER'S HOMECOMING by Cathy McDavid,
Sweetheart, Nevada
Harlequin American Romance

MAROONED WITH THE MAVERICK by Christine Rimmer,
Montana Mavericks
Harlequin Special Edition

CELEBRATION'S BRIDE by Nancy Robards Thompson,
Celebrations, Inc.
Harlequin Special Edition

*Look for these great Western reads AND MORE,
available wherever books are sold or visit*
www.Harlequin.com/Westerns

SUART0613HF

Another Callahan Cowboys story from
USA TODAY **bestselling author**

TINA LEONARD

Marriage isn't in Dante Callahan's short-term plans.
But Ana St. John is! After the gorgeous nanny
bodyguard—and woman of his fantasies—turns the
tables and seduces *him*, Dante is suddenly corralling
his inner wild man. Now Ana is having his baby…and
refusing to say "I do"!

He may be crazy for pulling out all stops to get Ana to
marry—but that's part of the fun of being a Callahan!

Branded by a Callahan

**Available July 1
from Harlequin® American Romance®.**

www.Harlequin.com

HAR75461

Meet THE CASH BROTHERS, six sexy rodeo cowboys. It takes a special woman to lasso one of these men!

Hardworking cowboy Johnny Cash has always been a protector to his little sister's best friend, sweet but tough cowgirl Shannon Douglas. It's pretty crazy for girls to ride bulls—but absolutely no way can he fall for the boss's daughter....

Johnny's protectiveness drives her crazy...the same way his kisses do. Her heart says he's the one—but her own stubborn streak might push him away.

The Cowboy Next Door

by Marin Thomas

Book one in THE CASH BROTHERS series

Available July 1
from Harlequin® American Romance®.

www.Harlequin.com

HAR75463